we'll
always
have
summer

Also by Jenny Han

Shug
Clara Lee and the Apple Pie Dream

The Summer I Turned Pretty
It's Not Summer Without You

To All the Boys I've Loved Before
P.S. I Still Love You
Always and Forever, Lara Jean

Cowritten with Siobhan Vivian

Burn for Burn
Fire with Fire
Ashes to Ashes

the summer i turned pretty
volume three

we'll
always
have
summer

JENNY HAN

SIMON & SCHUSTER BFYR

New York   London   Toronto   Sydney   New Delhi

SIMON & SCHUSTER BFYR

An imprint of Simon & Schuster Children's Publishing Division
1230 Avenue of the Americas, New York, New York 10020

For information about special discounts for bulk purchases, please contact Simon & Schuster Special Sales at 1-866-506-1949 or business@simonandschuster.com.
The Simon & Schuster Speakers Bureau can bring authors to your live event. For more information or to book an event, contact the Simon & Schuster Speakers Bureau at 1-866-248-3049 or visit our website at www.simonspeakers.com.
Also available in a SIMON & SCHUSTER BFYR hardcover edition
Interior design by Lucy Ruth Cummins
The text for this book is set in Bembo.

First SIMON & SCHUSTER BFYR paperback edition April 2012
20 19 18 17 16 15 14 13 12
The Library of Congress has cataloged the hardcover edition as follows:
Han, Jenny.
  We'll always have summer : a summer novel / Jenny Han.—1st ed.
    p. cm.
  Sequel to: It's not summer without you.
  Summary: The summer after her first year of college, Isobel "Belly" Conklin is faced with a choice between Jeremiah and Conrad Fisher, brothers she has always loved, when Jeremiah proposes marriage and Conrad confesses that he still loves her.
  ISBN 978-1-4169-9558-6 (hc)
  [1. Love—Fiction. 2. Brothers—Fiction. 3. Interpersonal relations—Fiction. 4. Beaches—Fiction. 5. Vacation homes—Fiction.] I. Title. II. Title: We will always have summer.
PZ7.H18944We 2011
[Fic]—dc22
2010046670
ISBN 978-1-4169-9559-3 (pbk)
ISBN 978-1-4169-9560-9 (eBook)

For my two Emilys:
Emily van Beek, you are my ambassador of quan
Emily Thomas Meehan, let's stay together forever
love, your girl

🐚 🐚 🐚

Acknowledgments

First, my sincerest thanks to Emily Meehan for seeing this book through. Many thanks also to Julia Maguire for not missing a beat, Lucy Ruth Cummins for another gorgeous cover, Justin Chanda and Anne Zafian for their steadfast support, and to the whole (frankly, amazing) S&S team. From sales to production to marketing to publicity, you guys are tops in my book. Thanks as always to Emily van Beek and Folio, to my Pippin family, and also to Siobhan Vivian, my first and finest reader.

On Wednesday nights when I was little, my mom and I would watch old musicals. It was our thing. Sometimes my dad or Steven would wander in and watch for a bit, but it was pretty much always my mother and me on the couch with a blanket and a bowl of sweet and salty popcorn, every Wednesday. We watched *The Music Man, West Side Story, Meet Me in St. Louis*, all of which I liked, *Singin' in the Rain*, which I really liked. But I loved none of them the way I loved *Bye Bye Birdie*. Of all the musicals, *Bye Bye Birdie* was my number one favorite. I watched it again and again, as many times as my mother could stand. Just like Kim MacAfee before me, I wanted to wear mascara and lipstick and heels and have that "happy grown-up female feeling," I wanted to hear boys whistle and know it was for me. I wanted to grow up and be just like Kim, because she got to have all of those things.

And after, when it was bedtime, I would sing, "We love you, Conrad, oh yes we do. We love you, Conrad, and we'll be true" into the bathroom mirror with a mouthful of toothpaste. I would sing my eight-nine-ten-year-old heart out. But I wasn't singing to Conrad Birdie. I was singing to *my* Conrad. Conrad Beck Fisher, the boy of my preteen dreams.

I've only ever loved two boys—both of them with the last name Fisher. Conrad was first, and I loved him in a way that you can really only do the first time around. It's the kind of love that doesn't know better and doesn't want to—it's dizzy and foolish and fierce. That kind of love is really a one-time-only thing.

And then there was Jeremiah. When I looked at Jeremiah, I saw past, present, and future. He didn't just know the girl I used to be. He knew the right-now me, and he loved me anyway.

My two great loves. I think I always knew I would be Belly Fisher one day. I just didn't know it was going to happen like this.

chapter *one*

When it's finals week and you've been studying for five hours straight, you need three things to get you through the night. The biggest Slurpee you can find, half cherry, half Coke. Pajama pants, the kind that have been washed so many times, they are tissue-paper thin. And finally, dance breaks. Lots of dance breaks. When your eyes start to close and all you want is your bed, dance breaks will get you through.

It was four in the morning, and I was studying for the last final of my freshman year at Finch University. I was camped out in my dorm library with my new best friend, Anika Johnson, and my old best friend, Taylor Jewel. Summer vacation was so close, I could almost taste it. Just five more days. I'd been counting down since April.

"Quiz me," Taylor commanded, her voice scratchy.

I opened my notebook to a random page. "Define *anima* versus *animus*."

Taylor chewed on her lower lip. "Give me a hint."

"Umm . . . think Latin," I said.

"I didn't take Latin! Is there going to be Latin on this exam?"

"No, I was just trying to give you a hint. Because in Latin boys' names end in -*us* and girls' names end in -*a*, and *anima* is feminine archetype and *animus* is masculine archetype. Get it?"

She let out a big sigh. "No. I'm probably going to fail."

Looking up from her notebook, Anika said, "Maybe if you stopped texting and started studying, you wouldn't."

Taylor glared at her. "I'm helping my big sister plan our end-of-year breakfast, so I have to be on call tonight."

"On call?" Anika looked amused. "Like a doctor?"

"Yes, just like a doctor," Taylor snapped.

"So, will it be pancakes or waffles?"

"French toast, thank you very much."

The three of us were all taking the same freshman psych class, and Taylor's and my exam was tomorrow, Anika's was the day after. Anika was my closest friend at school besides Taylor. Seeing as how Taylor was competitive by nature, it was a friendship that she was more than a little jealous of, not that she'd ever in a million years admit it.

My friendship with Anika was different from my

friendship with Taylor. Anika was laid-back and easy to be with. She wasn't quick to judge. More than all that, though, she gave *me* the space to be different. She hadn't known me my whole life, so she had no expectations or preconceptions. There was freedom in that. And she wasn't like any of my friends back home. She was from New York, and her father was a jazz musician and her mother was a writer.

A couple of hours later, the sun was rising and casting the room in a bluish light, and Taylor's head was down, while Anika was staring off into space like a zombie.

I rolled up two paper balls in my lap and threw them at my two friends. "Dance break," I sang out as I pressed play on my computer. I did a little shimmy in my chair.

Anika glared at me. "Why are you so chipper?"

"Because," I said, clapping my hands together, "in just a few hours, it will all be over." My exam wasn't until one in the afternoon, so my plan was to go back to my room and sleep for a couple of hours, then wake up with time to spare and study some more.

I overslept, but I still managed to get another hour of studying in. I didn't have time to go to the dining hall for breakfast, so I just drank a Cherry Coke from the vending machine.

The test was as hard as we had expected, but I was pretty sure I would get at least a B. Taylor was pretty sure she hadn't failed, which was good. Both of us were too tired to celebrate after, so we just high-fived and went our separate ways.

I headed back to my dorm room, ready to pass out until at least dinnertime, and when I opened the door, there was Jeremiah, asleep in my bed. He looked like a little boy when he slept, even with the stubble. He was stretched out on top of my comforter, his feet hanging over the edge of the bed, my stuffed polar bear hugged to his chest.

I took off my shoes and crawled into my twin, extra-long bed next to him. He stirred, opened his eyes, and said, "Hi."

"Hi," I said.

"How'd it go?"

"Pretty good."

"Good." He let go of Junior Mint and hugged me to him. "I brought you the other half of my sub from lunch."

"You're sweet," I said, burrowing my head in his shoulder.

He kissed my hair. "I can't have my girl skipping meals left and right."

"It was just breakfast," I said. As an afterthought, I added, "And lunch."

"Do you want my sub now? It's in my book bag."

Now that I thought about it, I was hungry, but I was also sleepy. "Maybe a little later," I said, closing my eyes.

Then he fell back to sleep, and I fell asleep too. When I woke up, it was dark out, Junior Mint was on the floor, and Jeremiah's arms were around me. He was still asleep.

We had started dating right before I began senior year of high school. "Dating" didn't feel like the right word for it. We were just together. It all happened so easily and so quickly that it felt like it had always been that way. One minute we were friends, then we were kissing, and then the next thing I knew, I was applying to the same college as him. I told myself and everyone else (including him, including my mother especially) that it was a good school, that it was only a few hours from home and it made sense to apply there, that I was keeping my options open. All of those things were true. But truest of all was that I just wanted to be near him. I wanted him for all seasons, not just summer.

Now here we were, lying next to each other in my dorm-room bed. He was a sophomore, and I was finishing up my freshman year. It was crazy how far we had come. We'd known each other our whole lives, and in some ways, it felt like a big surprise—in other ways it felt inevitable.

chapter two

Jeremiah's fraternity was throwing an end-of-year party. In less than a week we would all go home for the summer, and we wouldn't be back at Finch until the end of August. I had always loved summertime best of all, but now that I was finally going home, somehow it felt a little bittersweet. I was used to meeting Jeremiah in the dining hall for breakfast every morning and doing my laundry with him at his frat house late at night. He was good at folding my T-shirts.

This summer, he would be interning at his dad's company again, and I was going to waitress at a family restaurant called Behrs, the same as I did last summer. Our plan was to meet at the summer house in Cousins as often as we could. Last summer we hadn't made it out there once. We'd both been so busy with our jobs.

I took every shift I could to save money for school. All the while, I'd felt a little hollow inside, my first summer away from Cousins.

There were a few lightning bugs out. It was just getting dark, and it wasn't too hot of a night. I was wearing heels, which was stupid, since on a last-minute impulse I'd walked instead of taking the bus. I just figured it was the last time for a long time I'd walk across campus on a nice night like this.

I'd invited Anika and our friend Shay to come with me, but Anika had a party with her dance team, and Shay was already done with finals and had flown home to Texas. Taylor's sorority was having a mixer, so she wasn't coming either. It was just me and my sore feet.

I had texted Jeremiah to tell him I was on my way and that I was walking, so it would take me a little while. I had to keep stopping to adjust my shoes because they were cutting into the backs of my feet. Heels were dumb, I decided.

Halfway there, I saw him sitting on my favorite bench. He stood up when he saw me. "Surprise!"

"You didn't have to meet me," I said, feeling very happy he had. I sat down on the bench.

"You look hot," he said.

Even now, after being boyfriend and girlfriend for a whole two years, I still blushed a little when he said things like that. "Thanks," I said. I was wearing a sundress that

I had borrowed from Anika. It was white with little blue flowers and ruffly straps.

"That dress reminds me of *The Sound of Music*, but in a hot way."

"Thanks," I said again. *Did* the dress make me look like Fräulein Maria, I wondered? That didn't sound like a good thing. I smoothed down the straps a little.

A couple of guys I didn't recognize stopped and said hi to Jeremiah, but I stayed put on the bench so I could rest my feet.

When they were gone, he said, "Ready?"

I groaned. "My feet are killing me. Heels are dumb."

Jeremiah stooped down low and said, "Hop on, girl."

Giggling, I climbed on his back. I always giggled when he called me "girl." I couldn't help it. It was funny.

He hoisted me up and I put my arms around his neck. "Is your dad coming on Monday?" Jeremiah asked as we crossed the main lawn.

"Yeah. You're gonna help, right?"

"Come on, now. I'm carrying you across campus. I have to help you move, too?"

I swatted him on the head and he ducked. "Okay, okay," he said.

Then I blew a raspberry on his neck, and he yelped like a little girl. I laughed the whole way there.

chapter *three*

At Jeremiah's fraternity house, the doors were wide open and people were hanging out on the front lawn. Multicolored Christmas lights were haphazardly strung all over the place—on the mailbox, the front porch, even along the edge of the walkway. They had three inflatable kiddie pools set up that people were lounging in like they were in hot tubs. Guys were running around with Super Soakers and spraying beer into each other's mouths. Some of the girls were in their bikinis.

I hopped off Jeremiah's back and took my shoes off in the grass.

"The pledges did a nice job with this," Jeremiah said, nodding appreciatively at the kiddie pools. "Did you bring your suit?"

I shook my head.

"Want me to see if one of the girls has an extra?" he offered.

Quickly, I said, "No thanks."

I knew Jeremiah's fraternity brothers from hanging out at the house, but I didn't know the girls very well. Most of them were from Zeta Phi, Jeremiah's fraternity's sister sorority. That meant they had mixers and parties together, that kind of thing. Jeremiah had wanted me to rush Zeta Phi, but I'd said no. I told him it was because I couldn't afford the fees and paying extra to live in a sorority house, but it was really more that I was hoping to be friends with all kinds of girls, not just the ones I'd meet in a sorority. I wanted a broader college experience, like my mother was always saying. According to Taylor, Zeta Phi was for party girls and sluts, as opposed to her sorority, which was allegedly classier and more exclusive. And way more focused on community service, she'd added as an afterthought.

Girls kept coming up and hugging Jeremiah. They said hi to me, and I said hi back, then I went upstairs to put my bag in Jeremiah's room. On my way downstairs, I saw her.

Lacie Barone, wearing skinny jeans and a silky tank top and patent leather red heels that probably brought her up to five-four at most, talking to Jeremiah. Lacie was the social chair of Zeta Phi, and she was a junior—a year older than Jere, two years older than me. Her hair was dark brown, cut in a swishy bob, and she was petite. She was, by anybody's standards, hot. According to Taylor, she had a thing for Jeremiah. I told Taylor it didn't bother me one bit, and I meant it. Why should I care?

Of course girls would like Jeremiah. He was the kind of boy girls liked. But even a girl as pretty as Lacie didn't have anything on us. We were a couple years and years in the making. I knew him better than anyone, the same as he knew me, and I knew Jere would never look at another girl.

Jeremiah saw me then, and he waved at me to come over. I walked up to them and said, "Hey, Lacie."

"Hey," she said.

Pulling me toward him, Jeremiah said, "Lacie is gonna study abroad in Paris this fall." To Lacie, he said, "We want to go backpacking in Europe next summer."

Sipping her beer, she said, "That's cool. Which countries?"

"We're definitely going to France," Jeremiah said. "Belly speaks really fluent French."

"I actually don't," I told her, embarrassed. "I just took it in high school."

Lacie said, "Oh, I'm horrible too. I really just want to go and eat lots of cheese and chocolate."

She had a voice that was surprisingly husky for someone so small. I wondered if she smoked. She smiled at me, and I thought, Taylor was wrong about her, she was a nice girl.

When she left a few minutes later to get a drink, I said, "She's nice."

Jeremiah shrugged and said, "Yeah, she's cool. Want me to get you a drink?"

"Sure," I said.

He led me by the shoulders and planted me on the couch. "You sit right here. Don't move a muscle. I'll be right back."

I watched him make his way through the crowd, feeling proud I could call him mine. My boyfriend, my Jeremiah. The first boy I had ever fallen asleep next to. The first boy I ever told about the time I accidentally walked in on my parents doing it when I was eight. The first boy to go out and buy me Midol because my cramps were so bad, the first boy to paint my toenails, to hold my hair back when I threw up that time I got really drunk in front of all his friends, the first boy to write me a love note on the whiteboard hanging outside my dorm room.

YOU ARE THE MILK TO MY SHAKE,
forever and ever. Love, J.

He was the first boy I ever kissed. He was my best friend. More and more, I understood. This was the way it was supposed to be. He was the one. My one.

chapter *four*

It was later that night.

We were dancing. I had my arms around Jeremiah's neck, and the music was pulsing around us. I felt flushed and abuzz, from the dancing and from the alcohol. The room was packed with people, but when Jere looked at me, there was no one else. Just me and him.

He reached down and tucked a strand of hair behind my ear. He said something I couldn't hear.

"What?" I yelled.

He yelled, "Don't ever cut your hair, okay?"

"I have to! I'd look like—like a witch."

Jeremiah tapped his ear and said, "I can't hear you!"

"Witch!" I shook my hair around my face for emphasis and mimed stirring a cauldron and cackling.

"I like you witchy," he said in my ear. "How about just trims?"

I shouted, "I promise not to cut my hair short if you promise to give up your beard dream!"

He'd been talking about growing a beard ever since Thanksgiving, when some of his high school friends got a contest going to see who could grow it the longest. I'd told him no way, it reminded me too much of my dad.

"I'll consider it," he said, kissing me.

He tasted like beer, and I probably did too.

Then Jeremiah's frat brother Tom—also known as Redbird for reasons unknown to me—spotted us, and he came charging at Jeremiah like a bull. He was wearing his underwear and carrying a water bottle. And they weren't boxers, they were tighty whities. "Break it up, break it up!" he shouted.

They started messing around, and when Jeremiah got Tom in a headlock, Tom's water bottle of beer spilled all over me and Anika's dress.

"Sorry, sorry," he mumbled. When Tom was really drunk, he said everything twice.

"It's okay," I said, wringing out the skirt and trying not to look at the lower half of his body.

I left to go clean my dress in the bathroom, but there was a long line, so I went to the kitchen. People were doing body shots on the kitchen table; Jeremiah's frat brother Luke was licking salt out of a red-haired girl's belly button.

"Hey, Isabel," he said, looking up.

"Um, hey, Luke," I said. Then I spotted some girl throwing up in the sink, and I booked it out of there.

I headed to the upstairs bathroom. At the top of the staircase, I squeezed past a guy and a girl making out, and I accidentally stepped on the guy's hand. "I'm so sorry," I said, but he didn't seem to notice either way, since he had his other hand up the girl's shirt.

When I finally made it to the bathroom, I locked the door behind me and let out a little sigh of relief. This party was even wilder than usual. I guessed with the end of year upon us and finals over, everybody was letting loose. I was kind of glad Anika hadn't been able to come. It wouldn't be her scene—not that it was mine, either.

I dabbed liquid soap onto the wet marks and crossed my fingers it wouldn't stain. Someone tried to open the door, and I called out, "Just a sec."

As I stood there, dabbing at the dress, I heard girls on the other side talking. I wasn't really paying attention until I heard Lacie's voice. I heard her say, "He looks hot tonight, right?"

Another voice said, "He always looks hot."

She was slurring as she said, "Hell yeah he does."

The other girl said, "I'm so jealous you got to hook up with him."

In a singsong voice, Lacie said, "Whatever happens in Cabo stays in Cabo."

I felt dizzy all of a sudden. I leaned my back against

the bathroom door to steady myself. There was no way she was talking about Jeremiah. No way.

Someone banged on the door, and I jumped.

Without thinking, I opened it. Lacie's hand flew to her mouth when she saw me. The look on her face was like a punch in the stomach. I felt physical pain. I could hear the other girls' sharp intakes of breath, but it all felt far away. I felt like I was sleepwalking as I moved past her and the girls and down the hallway.

I couldn't believe it. It couldn't be true. Not my Jere.

I went to his room and locked the door behind me. I sat on his bed, knees curled into my chest, going over it in my head. *Whatever happens in Cabo stays in Cabo.* The look on Lacie's face, the way the other girls gasped. It played in my head like a movie, over and over. The two of them talking tonight. The way he'd shrugged when I said she was nice.

I had to know for sure. I had to hear it from Jeremiah.

I left his room and went looking for him. As I searched, I could feel the shock turning into anger. I pushed my way through the crowd. One drunk girl slurred, "Hey!" when I stepped on her foot, but I didn't stop to say "excuse me."

I finally found him standing around outside drinking beer with his frat buddies. From the open door, I said, "I need to talk to you."

"Just a sec, Bells," he said.

"No. Now."

The guys all started cracking up and going, "Oooh, somebody's in trouble." "Fisher's so whipped."

I waited.

Jeremiah must have seen something in my eyes, because he followed me inside, up the stairs, and into his bedroom. I shut the door behind me.

"What's going on?" he asked me, looking all concerned.

I practically spat the words out. "Did you hook up with Lacie Barone during spring break?"

Jeremiah's face turned white. "What?"

"Did you hook up with her?"

"Belly—"

"I knew it," I whispered. "I knew it."

Even though I didn't know it, not really. I didn't know anything.

"Hold on, just hold on."

"Hold on?" I screamed. "Oh my God, Jere. Oh my God."

I sank onto the floor. My legs couldn't even hold me up.

Jeremiah kneeled down beside me and tried to help me up, but I slapped his hands away. "Don't touch me!"

He got down on the floor next to me, his head hanging between his knees. "Belly, it was when we were on that break. When we were broken up." I stared at him.

Our so-called breakup had lasted all of a week. It wasn't even a real breakup, not for me. I always assumed we would get back together. I had cried the whole week, while he had been in Cabo kissing Lacie Barone.

"You knew we weren't really broken up! You knew it wasn't real!"

Miserably, he said, "How was I supposed to know that?"

"If I knew it, you should have known it!"

He swallowed, and his Adam's apple bobbed up and down. "Lacie kept following me around all week. She wouldn't leave me alone. I swear to you, I didn't want to hook up with her. It just happened." His voice trailed off.

I felt so dirty inside hearing him say that. Just disgusted. I didn't want to think about the two of them, didn't want to picture it. "Be quiet," I said. "I don't want to hear it."

"It was a mistake."

"A mistake? You call that a mistake? A mistake is when you left my shower shoes in the shower and they got all mildewy and I had to throw them out. That's a mistake, you jerk." I burst into tears.

He didn't say anything. He just sat there and took it, his head hanging down.

"I don't even know who you are anymore." My stomach lurched. "I think I'm going to be sick."

Jeremiah got me the wastebasket by his bed and I threw up, heaving and crying. He tried to rub my back, but I jerked away from him. "Don't touch me," I mumbled, wiping my mouth with the back of my arm.

It didn't make sense. None of it. This wasn't the

Jeremiah I knew. My Jeremiah would never hurt me like this. He would never so much as look at another girl. My Jeremiah was true and strong and steady. I didn't know who this person was.

"I'm sorry," he said. "I'm really sorry."

Jeremiah was crying now too. Good, I thought. Hurt like you've hurt me.

"I want to be totally honest with you, Belly. I don't want any more secrets." He really broke down then, crying hard.

I went totally still.

"We had sex."

Before I knew it, my hand was striking his face. I slapped him as hard as I could. I wasn't even thinking, I was just doing. My hand left a splotchy red imprint on his right cheek.

We stared at each other. I couldn't believe I had hit him, and neither could he. The shock was just beginning to register on his face, and I probably had the same look on mine. I had never hit anyone before.

Rubbing his cheek, he said, "I'm so sorry."

I cried harder. I had pictured them hooking up, making out. I hadn't even considered sex. I was so stupid.

He said, "It didn't mean anything. I swear to you, it didn't."

He tried to touch my arm, and I flinched. Wiping my cheeks, I said, "Maybe to you sex doesn't mean anything.

But it means something to me, and you knew that. You've ruined everything. I'll never trust you again."

He tried to pull me toward him, but I pushed him away. Desperately, he said, "I'm telling you, the thing with Lacie didn't mean anything."

"It means something to *me*. And it obviously meant something to her."

"I'm not in love with her!" he cried out. "I'm in love with you!"

Jeremiah crawled over to where I was. He put his arms around my knees. "Don't leave," he begged. "Please don't leave."

I tried to shake him off, but he was strong. He clung to me like I was a raft and he was at sea.

"I love you so much," he said, his whole body shaking. "It's always been you, Belly."

I wanted to keep screaming and crying and somehow find a way out of this. But I didn't see a way. Looking down at him, I felt like I was made of stone. He had never disappointed me before. For him to do it now made it that much harder, because I hadn't seen it coming. It was hard to believe that just a few short hours ago he'd carried me across campus on his back and I'd loved him more than ever.

"We can't get it back," I said, and I said it to hurt him. "What we were, it's gone. We lost it tonight."

Desperately, he said, "Yes, we can. I know we can."

I shook my head. The tears had started again, but I didn't want to cry anymore, especially not in front of him. Or with him. I didn't want to feel sad. I didn't want to feel anything. I wiped my face again and stood up, "I'm leaving."

He rose to his feet unsteadily. "Wait!"

I pushed past him and grabbed my bag from his bed. Then I was out the door, running down the stairs and outside. I ran all the way to the bus stop, my bag banging against my shoulder, my heels clacking against the pavement. I almost tripped and fell, but I made it. I caught the bus just as the last person was getting on, and we drove off. I didn't look back to see if Jeremiah had followed me.

My roommate, Jillian, had gone home for the summer earlier that day, so at least I had the room to myself and could cry alone. Jeremiah kept calling and texting, so I turned my phone off. But before I went to bed, I turned it back on again so I could see what he wrote me.

I'm so ashamed of myself.
Please talk to me.
I love you and I always will.

I cried harder.

chapter *five*

When we broke up in April, it really did come out of nowhere. Yes, we'd had little fights here and there, but you could hardly even call them fights.

Like, there was this time Shay was having a party at her godmother's country house. She invited a ton of people, and she said I could bring Jeremiah, too. We were gonna get dressed up and dance outside all night long. We'd all just crash there for the weekend, Shay said—it would be a blast. I was just happy to be included. I told Jeremiah about it, and he said he had an intramural soccer game but I should go anyway. I said, "Can't you just miss it? It's not like it's a real game." It was a bitchy thing to say, but I said it, and I meant it.

That was our first fight. Not a real fight, not like yelling or anything, but he was mad and so was I.

We always hung out with his friends. In a way it made sense. He already had them, and I was still forming mine. It took time to get close to people, and with me at his frat house all the time, the girls on my hall were bonding without me. I felt like I had given something up without even realizing it. When Shay invited me, that meant a lot, and I wanted it to mean something to Jere, too.

And there were other things, too, that annoyed me. Things I'd never known about Jeremiah, things I couldn't have known from only seeing him in the summer at the beach house. Like how obnoxious he was when he smoked weed with his suitemates and they ate pineapple-and-ham pizza and listened to "Gangsta's Paradise" by Coolio and they would laugh for, like, an hour.

Also his seasonal allergies. I'd never seen him in the springtime, so I didn't know he had them.

He called me, sneezing like crazy, all stuffed up and pitiful. "Can you come over and hang out with me?" he asked, blowing his nose. "And can you bring more Kleenex? And orange juice?"

I bit my lip to keep from saying, You have allergies, not swine flu.

I'd gone over to his frat house the day before. He and his roommate played video games while I did my homework. Then we watched a Kung Fu movie and ordered Indian food, even though I didn't really like to eat Indian food because it gave me an upset stomach after. Jeremiah said that when his allergies got really bad, Indian food was the only thing that would make him feel better. I ate naan and rice and felt pissed while Jeremiah scarfed down chicken tikka masala and watched his movie. He could be really oblivious sometimes, and I had to wonder if it was on purpose.

"I really want to come over, but I have a paper that's due tomorrow," I said, trying to sound conflicted about it. "So I probably shouldn't. Sorry."

"Well, I guess I could go there," he said. "I'll take a ton of Benedryl and sleep while you write. Then maybe we can order Indian food again."

"Yeah," I said, sourly. "We could do that." At least I wouldn't have to take the bus. But I would have to go to the hall bathroom and get a roll of toilet paper, because Jillian would be pissed if Jeremiah used all her Kleenex again.

I didn't know then that all of that was setting the stage for our first real fight. We had one of those screaming and crying kind of fights, the kind I promised myself I would never have. I'd heard Jillian have them over the phone, girls on my hall, Taylor. I never thought it would be me. I thought Jeremiah and I understood each other too well, had known each other too long, for that kind of fight.

A fight is like a fire. You think you have it under control, you think you can stop it whenever you want, but before you know it, it's a living, breathing thing and there's no controlling it and you were a fool to think you could.

At the last minute, Jeremiah and his fraternity brothers decided to go to Cabo over spring break. They'd found some insane deal on the Internet.

I was already planning on going home over the break. My mom and I were going to go into the city and watch a ballet, and Steven would be at home too. So I wanted to be at home, I really did. But as I watched Jeremiah book his trip, I felt more and more resentful. He was supposed to be going home too. Now that Conrad was in California, Mr. Fisher was pretty much alone. Jeremiah had said he wanted to go and spend some time with him, maybe visit Susannah's grave together. We'd also talked about going to Cousins for a couple of days. Jeremiah knew how much I wanted to go to Cousins. He knew how much it meant to me. I'd done more growing up in that house than I had in my own. And with Susannah gone, it felt even more important that we kept going back.

Now he was going to Cabo. Without me.

"Do you really think you should be going to Cabo?" I asked him. He was sitting at his desk, hunched over the computer and typing away. I was sitting on his bed.

He looked up, surprised. "It's too good of a deal to pass up. Besides, all my brothers are going. I can't miss out."

"Yeah, but I thought you were gonna go home and hang out with your dad."

"I can do that over summer break."

"Summer's still months away." I crossed my arms then uncrossed them.

Jeremiah frowned. "What's this about? Are you worried about me going on spring break without you?"

I could feel my cheeks redden. "No! You can go wherever you want, I don't care. I just think that it would be nice if you spent some time with your dad. And your mom's headstone is up. I thought you wanted to go see it."

"Yeah, I do, but I can do all that after school's out. You can come with me." He peered at me. "Are you jealous?"

"No!"

He was grinning now. "Worried about all the wet T-shirt contests?"

"No!" I hated that he was making this into a joke. It was infuriating, being the only one who was mad.

"If you're so worried, then just come with us. It'll be fun."

He did not say, If you are worried, you shouldn't be. He said, *If you are worried, you should come with us.* I knew he didn't mean it that way, but it still bothered me.

"You know I can't afford it. Besides, I don't want to go to Cabo with you and your 'bros.' I'm not going to go and be the only girlfriend and drag down your party."

"You wouldn't be. Josh's girlfriend, Alison, is going to be there," Jeremiah said.

So Alison had been invited and not me? I sat up straight. "Alison's going with you guys?"

"It's not like that. Alison's going with her sorority. They're getting a bunch of rooms at the same resort as us. That's how we found out about the deal. But it's not like we'll be hanging out with them all the time. We're gonna do guy stuff, like off-road racing in the desert. Rent some ATVs, go rappelling, stuff like that."

I stared at him. "So while you race around with your buddies in the desert, you want me to hang out with a bunch of girls I don't know?"

He rolled his eyes. "You know Alison. You guys were beer-pong partners in our house tournament."

"Whatever. I'm not going to Cabo. I'm going home. My mom misses me." What I didn't say was, your dad misses you too.

When Jeremiah just shrugged, like, Have it your way, I thought, oh, what the hell, I'll say it. "Your dad misses you too."

"Oh my God. Belly, just admit that this isn't about my dad. You're paranoid about me going on spring break without you."

"Why don't you admit that you didn't want me to go in the first place, then?"

He hesitated. I saw him hesitate. "Fine. Yeah, I wouldn't mind if this was just a guys' trip."

Standing up, I said, "Well, it sounds like there will be plenty of girls there. Have fun with the Zetas."

Now his neck started to turn a dull red. "If you don't trust me by now, I don't know what to tell you. I've never done anything to make you question me. And Belly, I really don't need you guilt tripping me about my dad."

I started putting my shoes on, and I was so mad, my hands shook as I tried to lace up my sneakers. "I can't even believe how selfish you are."

"Me? I'm the selfish one now?" He shook his head, his lips tight. He opened his mouth like he was going to say something, but then he closed it.

"Yes, you are definitely the selfish one in this relationship. It's always about you, your friends, your stupid fraternity. Have I told you I think your fraternity is stupid? Because I do."

In a low voice, he said, "What's so stupid about it?"

"It's just a bunch of entitled rich guys spending their parents' money, cheating on tests with your test bank, going to class wasted."

Looking hurt, he said, "We're not all like that."

"I didn't mean you."

"Yeah, you did. What, just because I'm not pre-med, that makes me this lazy frat guy?"

"Don't put your inferiority complex on me," I said. I

said it without thinking. It was something I had thought before but never voiced. Conrad was the one who was pre-med. Conrad was the one at Stanford, working a part-time job at a lab. Jeremiah was the one who told people he majored in beerology.

He stared. "What the hell does that mean, 'inferiority complex'?"

"Forget it," I said. Too late, I could see things had gone farther than I had intended. I wanted to take it all back.

"If you think I'm so stupid and selfish and wasteful, why are you even with me?"

Before I could answer, before I could say, You're not stupid or selfish or wasteful, before I could end the fight, Jeremiah said, "Fuck it. I won't waste your time anymore. Let's end it now."

And I said, "Fine."

I grabbed my book bag, but I didn't leave right away. I was waiting for him to stop me. But he didn't.

I cried the whole way home. I couldn't believe that we had broken up. It didn't feel real. I expected Jeremiah to call me that night. It was a Friday. He left for Cabo on Sunday morning, and he didn't call then, either.

My spring break consisted of me moping around the house, eating chips, and crying. Steven said, "Chill out. The only reason he hasn't called you is that it's too expensive to make a call from Mexico. You guys will be back together by next week, guaranteed."

I was pretty sure he was right. Jeremiah just needed some space. Okay, that was fine. When he got back, I would go to him and tell him how sorry I was, and I would fix things, and it would be like it never happened.

Steven was right. We did get back together a week later. I did go to him and apologize, and he apologized too. I never asked him if anything happened in Cabo. It wouldn't even have occurred to me to wonder. This was a boy who had loved me my whole life, and I was a girl who believed in that love. In that boy.

Jere brought me back a shell bracelet. Little white puka shells. It had made me so happy. Because I knew that he had been thinking of me, that he had missed me as much as I had missed him. He knew like I knew that it wasn't over between us, that it would never be over. He spent that whole week after spring break in my room, hanging out with me and not his fraternity brothers. It drove my roommate Jillian crazy, but I didn't care. I felt closer to him than ever. I missed him even when he was in class.

But now I knew the truth. He bought me that stupid cheap bracelet because he felt guilty. And I was so desperate to make up, I hadn't seen it.

chapter *six*

When I closed my eyes, I saw the two of them, together, kissing in a hot tub. On the beach. In some club. Lacie Barone probably knew tricks and moves I'd never even heard of. But of course she did.

I was still a virgin.

I'd never had sex before, not with Jeremiah, not with anybody. When I was younger, I used to picture my first time with Conrad. It wasn't that I was still waiting for him. It wasn't that at all. I was just waiting for the perfect moment. I wanted it to feel special, to feel exactly right.

I'd pictured us finally doing it at the beach house, with the lights off and candles everywhere so I wouldn't feel shy. I'd pictured how gentle Jeremiah would be, how sweet. Lately I had been feeling more and more ready. I had thought this summer, the two of us back at Cousins—I thought that would be it.

It was humiliating thinking about it now, how naive I'd been. I'd thought he would wait as long as it took for me to be ready. I really believed that.

But how could we be together now? When I thought of him with her, Lacie, who was older and sexier and more worldly than I'd ever be, at least in my mind—it hurt so bad it was hard to breathe. The fact that she knew him in a way I didn't yet, had experienced something with him that I hadn't, that felt like the biggest betrayal of all.

A month ago, around the anniversary of his mom's death, we were lying in Jeremiah's twin bed. He rolled over and looked at me, and his eyes were so like Susannah's, I reached out my hand and covered them.

"Sometimes it hurts to look at you," I said. I loved that I could say that and he knew exactly what I meant.

"Close your eyes," he told me.

I did, and he came up close so we were face-to-face and I could feel his Crest breath warm on my cheek. We wrapped our legs around each other. I was overcome with this sudden need to keep him close to me always. "Do you think it will always be like this?" I asked him.

"How else would it be?" he asked.

We fell asleep that way. Like kids. Totally innocent.

We could never go back to that. How could we? It was all tainted now. Everything from March to now, it was tainted.

chapter *seven*

When I woke up the next morning, my eyes were so puffy, they were practically swollen shut. I splashed cold water on my face, but it didn't really help. I brushed my teeth. And then I went back to bed. I'd wake up and hear people moving out of the dorms, and then I'd just fall back to sleep. I should have been packing, but all I wanted to do was sleep. I slept all day. I woke up again when it was dark out, and I didn't turn on the lights. I just lay in bed until I fell asleep again.

It was late afternoon the next day when I finally got up. When I say "got up," I mean "sat up." I finally sat up in my bed. I was thirsty. I felt wrung dry from all the crying. This propelled me to actually get out of bed and walk the five feet over to the mini fridge and take one of the bottled waters Jillian had left behind.

Looking across the room at her empty bed and empty walls made me feel even more depressed. Last night I wanted to be alone. Today I thought I would go out of my mind if I didn't talk to another person.

I went down the hall to Anika's room. The first thing she said when she saw me was, "What's wrong?"

I sat on her bed and hugged her pillow to my chest. I had come to her wanting to talk, wanting to get it out, but now it was hard to say the words. I felt ashamed. Of him and for him. All my friends loved Jeremiah. They thought he was practically perfect. I knew that as soon as I told Anika, all of that would be gone. This would be real. For some reason, I still wanted to protect him.

"Iz, what happened?"

I'd really thought I was done crying, but a few tears leaked out anyway. I went ahead and said it. "Jeremiah cheated on me."

Anika sank onto the bed. "Shut the front door," she breathed. "When? With who?"

"With Lacey Barone, that girl in his sister sorority. During spring break. When we were broken up."

She nodded, taking this in.

"I'm so mad at him," I said. "For hooking up with another girl and then not telling me all this time. Not telling is the same as lying. I feel so stupid."

Anika handed me the box of tissues on her desk. "Girl, you let yourself feel whatever you need to feel," she said.

I blew my nose. "I feel . . . like maybe I don't know him like I thought I did. I feel like I can't trust him ever again."

"Keeping a secret like that from the person you love is probably the worst part," Anika said.

"You don't think the actual cheating is the worst part?"

"No. I mean, yeah, that is horrible. But he should have just told you. It was turning it into a secret that gave it power."

I was silent. I had a secret too. I hadn't told anyone, not even Anika or Taylor. I had told myself that it was because it wasn't important, and then I had put it out of my mind.

The past couple of years, I sometimes pulled out a memory I had of Conrad and looked at it, admired it, sort of in the same way I looked at my old shell collection. There was pleasure in just touching each shell, the ridges, the cool smoothness. Even after Jeremiah and I started dating, every once in a while, sitting in class or waiting for the bus or trying to fall asleep, I would pull out an old memory. The first time I ever beat him in a swimming race. The time he taught me how to dance. The way he used to wet down his hair in the mornings.

But there was one memory in particular, one I didn't let myself touch. It wasn't allowed.

chapter *eight*

It was the day after Christmas. My mother had gone on a weeklong trip to Turkey, a trip she'd had to postpone twice—once when Susannah's cancer came out of remission and then again after Susannah died. My father was with his girlfriend Linda's family in Washington, D.C. Steven was on a ski trip with some friends from school. Jeremiah and Mr. Fisher were visiting relatives in New York.

And me? I was at home, watching *A Christmas Story* on TV for the third time. I had on my Christmas pajamas, the ones Susannah had sent me a couple of years back—they were red flannel pjs with a jaunty mistletoe print, and they were way too long in the leg. Part of the fun of wearing them was rolling up the sleeves and ankles. I had just finished my dinner—a frozen pepperoni pizza and the rest of the sugar cookies a student had baked for my mother.

I was starting to feel like Kevin in *Home Alone*. Eight o'clock on a Saturday night, and I was dancing around the living room to "Rockin' Around the Christmas Tree," feeling sorry for myself. My fall-semester grades had been eh. My whole family was gone. I was eating frozen pizza alone. And when Steven saw me that first day back home, the first thing out of his mouth was, "Wow, freshman fifteen, huh?" I had punched him in the arm, and he said he was kidding, but he wasn't kidding. I had gained ten pounds in four months. I guessed eating hot wings and ramen and Dominos pizza at four in the morning with the boys will do that to a girl. But so what? The freshman fifteen was a rite of passage.

I went to the downstairs bathroom and slapped my cheeks like Kevin does in the movie. "So what!" I yelled.

I wasn't going to let it get me down. Suddenly I had an idea. I ran upstairs and started throwing things into my backpack—the novel my mom had bought me for Christmas, leggings, thick socks. Why should I be at home alone when I could be at my favorite place in the world?

Fifteen minutes later, after I rinsed off my dinner dishes and turned off all the lights, I was in Steven's car. His car was nicer than mine, and what he didn't know wouldn't hurt him. Besides, that was what he got for bringing up the freshman fifteen.

I was heading to Cousins, rocking out to "Please Come Home for Christmas" (the Bon Jovi version, of course) and snacking on chocolate-covered pretzels with red and green sprinkles (another gift for my mother). I knew I had made the right decision. I would be at the Cousins house in no time. I would light a fire, I would make some hot chocolate to go with my pretzels, I would wake up in the morning to a winter beach. Of course I loved the beach during the summer more, but the winter beach held its own special kind of charm for me. I decided I wouldn't tell anyone I'd gone. When everyone came back from their trips, it would be my little secret.

I did make it to Cousins in no time. The highway had been pretty much deserted, and I practically flew there. As I pulled into the driveway, I let out a big whoop. It was good to be back. This was my first time at the house in over a year.

I found the spare set of keys right where they always were—under the loose floorboard on the deck. I felt giddy as I stepped inside and turned on the lights.

The house was freezing cold, and it was a lot harder to get a fire going than I thought it would be. I gave up pretty quickly, and I made myself hot chocolate while I waited for the heat to get working. Then I brought down a bunch of blankets from the linen closet and got all cozy on the couch underneath them, with my chocolate-covered pretzels and my mug of hot chocolate. *How the Grinch Stole Christmas* was on, and I fell asleep to the sound of the Whos in Whoville singing "Welcome Christmas."

I woke up to the sound of someone breaking into the house. I heard banging on the door and then someone messing with the doorknob. At first I just lay there under my blankets, scared out of my mind and trying not to breathe too loud. I kept thinking, oh my God, oh my God, it's just like in *Home Alone*. What would Kevin do? What would Kevin do? Kevin would probably booby-trap the front hall, but there was no time for any of that.

And then the burglar called out, "Steven? Are you in there?"

I thought, oh my God, the other robber is already in the house and his name is Steven!

I hid under the blanket, and then I thought, Kevin would not hide under a blanket. He would protect his house.

I took the brass poker from the fireplace and my cell phone, and I crept over to the foyer. I was too scared to look out the window, and I didn't want him to see me, so I just pressed my body up against the door and listened hard, my finger on the number nine.

"Steve, open up. It's me."

My heart nearly stopped beating. I knew that voice. It was not the voice of a burglar. It was Conrad.

I flung the door open. It really was him. I gazed at him, and he gazed back. I didn't know it would feel that way to see him again. Heart in my throat, hard to breathe. For those couple of seconds, I forgot everything and there was just him.

He was wearing a winter coat I had never seen before, camel colored, and he was sucking on a mini candy cane. It fell out of his mouth. "What in the world?" he said, his mouth still open.

When I hugged him, he smelled like peppermint and Christmas.

His cheek was cold against mine. "Why are you holding a poker?"

I stepped back. "I thought you were a burglar."

"Of course you did."

He followed me back to the living room and sat in the chair opposite the couch. He still had that shocked look on his face. "What are you doing here?"

I shrugged and set the poker on the coffee table. My adrenaline rush was fading fast, and I was starting to feel pretty silly. "I was all alone at home, and I just felt like coming. What are *you* doing here? I didn't even know you were coming back."

Conrad was in California now. I hadn't seen him since he'd transferred the year before. He had some scruff on his face, like he hadn't shaved in a couple of days. It looked soft, though, not prickly. He looked tan, too, which I thought was weird, seeing how it was winter, and then I remembered that he went to school in California, where it was always sunny.

"My dad sent me a ticket at the last minute. It took us forever to land, because of the snow, so I got here late. Since Jere and my dad are still in New York, I figured I'd just come here." He squinted at me.

"What?" I asked, feeling self-conscious all of a sudden. I tried to smooth down the back of my hair—it was all fuzzy from being slept on. Discreetly, I touched the corners of my mouth. Had I been drooling?

"You have chocolate all over your face."

I wiped at my mouth with the back of my hand. "No, I don't," I lied. "It's probably just dirt."

Amused, he raised his eyebrows at the near-empty can of chocolate-covered pretzels. "What, did you just put your whole head in it to save time?"

"Shut it," I said, but I couldn't help smiling.

The only light in the room was from the flickering TV. It was so surreal, being with him like this. A truly random twist of what felt like fate. I shivered and drew my blankets closer to me.

Taking off his coat, he said, "Want me to start a fire?"

Right away, I said, "Yes! I couldn't get it going for some reason."

"It takes a special touch," he said in his arrogant way. I knew by now it was only posturing.

It was all so familiar. We had been here before, just like this, only two Christmases ago. So much had happened since then. He had a whole new life now, and so did I. Still, in some ways, it was like no time or distance had passed between us. In some ways, it felt the same.

Maybe he was thinking the same thing, because he said, "It might be too late for a fire. I think I'm just gonna go crash." Abruptly, he stood up and headed for the staircase. Then he turned back and asked, "Are you sleeping down here?"

"Yup," I said. "Snug as a bug in a rug."

When he reached the staircase, Conrad stopped and then said, "Merry Christmas, Belly. It's really good to see you."

"You too."

The next morning, right when I woke up, I had this funny feeling that he had already left. I don't know why. I ran over to the stairs to check, and just as I was coming around the banister, I tripped over my pajama pants and fell flat on my back, banging my head along the way.

I lay there with tears in my eyes, staring up at the ceiling. The pain was unreal. Then Conrad's head popped up above me. "Are you okay?" he asked, his mouth full of food, cereal probably. He tried to help me sit up, but I waved him off.

"Leave me alone," I mumbled, hoping that if I just blinked fast enough, my tears would dry up.

"Are you hurt? Can you move?"

"I thought you were gone," I said.

"Nope. Still here." He knelt down beside me. "Just let me try and lift you up."

I shook my head no.

Conrad got down on the floor next to me, and we both lay there on the wooden floor like we were about to start making snow angels. "How bad does it hurt, on a scale of one to ten? Does it feel like you pulled something?"

"On a scale of one to ten . . . it hurts an eleven."

"You're such a baby when it comes to pain," he said, but he sounded worried.

"I am not." I was about to prove him right. Even I could hear how teary I sounded.

"Hey, that fall you took was no joke. It was just like how animals slip and fall in cartoons, like with a banana peel."

Suddenly I didn't feel like crying anymore. "Are you calling me an animal?" I demanded, turning my head to look at him. He was trying to keep a straight face, but the corners of his mouth kept turning up. Then he turned his head to look at me, and we both started laughing. I laughed so hard my back hurt worse.

Mid-laugh, I stopped and said, "Ow."

He sat up and said, "I'm gonna pick you up and bring you over to the couch."

"No," I protested weakly. "I'm too heavy for you. I'll get up in a minute, just leave me here for now."

Conrad frowned, and I could tell he was offended. "I know I can't bench-press my body weight like Jere, but I can pick up a girl, Belly."

I blinked. "It's not that. I'm heavier than you think. You know, freshman fifteen or whatever." My face got hot, and I momentarily forgot about how badly my back hurt or how weird it was that he'd brought up Jere. I just felt embarrassed.

In a quiet voice, he said, "Well, you look the same to me." Then, very gently, he scooped me off the floor and into his arms. I held on with one arm around his neck, and said, "It was more like ten. Freshman ten."

He said, "Don't worry. I've got you."

He carried me over to the couch and set me down. "I'm gonna get you some Advil. That should help a little."

Looking up at him, I had this sudden thought.

Oh my God. I still love you.

I'd thought my feelings for Conrad were safely tucked away, like my old Rollerblades and the little gold watch my dad bought me when I first learned how to tell time.

But just because you bury something, that doesn't mean it stops existing. Those feelings, they'd been there all along. All that time. I had to just face it. He was a part of my DNA. I had brown hair and I had freckles and I would always have Conrad in my heart. He would inhabit just that tiny piece of it, the little-girl part that still believed in musicals, but that was it. That was all he got. Jeremiah would have everything else—the present me and the future me. That was what was important. Not the past.

Maybe that was how it was with all first loves. They own a little piece of your heart, always. Conrad at twelve, thirteen, fourteen, fifteen, sixteen, even seventeen years old. For the rest of my life, I would think of him fondly, the way you do your first pet, the first car you drove. Firsts were important. But I was pretty sure lasts were even more important. And Jeremiah, he was going to be my last and my every and my always.

Conrad and I spent the rest of that day together but not together. He started a fire, and then he read at the kitchen table while I watched *It's a Wonderful Life*. For lunch, we had canned tomato soup and the rest of my chocolate-covered pretzels. Then he went for a run on the beach and I settled in for *Casablanca*. I was wiping tears from the corners of my eyes with my T-shirt sleeve when he came back. "This movie makes my heart hurt," I croaked.

Taking off his fleece, Conrad said, "Why? It had a happy ending. She was better off with Laszlo."

I looked at him in surprise. "You've seen *Casablanca*?"

"Of course. It's a classic."

"Well, obviously you weren't paying that close of

attention, because Rick and Ilsa are meant for each other."

Conrad snorted. "Their little love story is nothing compared to the work Laszlo was doing for the Resistance."

Blowing my nose with a napkin, I said, "For a young guy, you're way too cynical."

He rolled his eyes. "And for a supposedly grown girl, you're way too emotional." He headed for the stairs.

"Robot!" I yelled at his back. "Tin man!"

I heard him laughing as he closed the bathroom door.

The next morning, Conrad was gone. He left just like I thought he'd leave. No good-bye, no nothing. Just gone, like a ghost. Conrad, the Ghost of Christmas Past.

Jeremiah called me when I was on the way back home from Cousins. He asked what I was doing, and I told him I was driving home, but I didn't tell him where I was driving from. It was a split-second decision. At the time I didn't know why I lied. I just knew I didn't want him to know.

I decided Conrad was right after all. Ilsa was meant to be with Laszlo. That was the way it was always supposed to end. Rick was nothing but a tiny piece of her past, a piece that she would always treasure, but that was all, because history is just that. History.

chapter *nine*

After I left Anika's room, I turned on my phone. There were texts and e-mails from Jeremiah, and they kept coming. I got under my covers and read them all, each and every one. Then I reread them, and when I was done, I finally wrote him back and said, *Give me some space.* He wrote *OK*, and that was the last text I got from him that day. I still kept checking my phone to see if there was anything from him, and when there wasn't, I was disappointed, even though I knew I didn't have a right to be. I wanted him to leave me alone, and I wanted him to keep trying to fix things. But if I didn't know what I wanted, how could he possibly?

I stayed in my room, packing up. I was hungry, and I still had meals left on my meal card, but I was afraid I might run into Lacie on campus. Or worse, Jeremiah. Still, it was good to have something to do and to be able to turn the music on loud without having to hear my roommate Jillian complain.

When I couldn't take the hunger anymore, I called Taylor and told her everything. She screamed so loud, I had to hold the phone away from my ear. She came right over with a black-bean burrito and a strawberry-banana smoothie. She kept shaking her head and saying, "That Zeta Phi slut."

"It wasn't just her, it was him, too," I said, between bites of my burrito.

"Oh, I know. Just you wait. I'm gonna drag my nails across his face when I see him. I'll leave him so scarred, no girl will ever hook up with him again." She inspected her manicured nails like they were artillery. "When I go to the salon tomorrow, I'm gonna tell Danielle to make them sharp."

My heart swelled. There are some things only a friend who's known you your whole life can say, and instantly, I felt a little better. "You don't have to scar him."

"But I want to." She hooked her pinky finger with mine. "Are you okay?"

I nodded. "Better, now that you're here."

When I was sucking down the last of my smoothie, Taylor asked me, "Do you think you'll take him back?"

I was surprised and really relieved not to hear any judgment in her voice. "What would you do?" I asked her.

"It's up to you."

"I know, but . . . would *you* take him back?"

"Under ordinary circumstances, no. If some guy cheated on me while we were on a break, if he so much as looked at another girl, no. He'd be donzo." She chewed on her straw. "But Jeremy's not some guy. You have a history together."

"What happened to all that talk about scarring him?"

"Don't get it twisted, I hate him to death right now. He effed up in a colossal way. But he'll never be just some guy, not to you. That's a fact."

I didn't say anything. But I knew she was right.

"I could still round up my sorority sisters and go slash his tires tonight." Taylor bumped my shoulder. "Hmm? Whaddyathink?"

She was trying to make me laugh. It worked. I laughed for the first time in what felt like a long time.

chapter *ten*

After our fight the summer before senior year, I really thought that Taylor and I would make up fast, the way we always did. I thought it would blow over in a week, tops. Because what were we really even mad about? Sure, we both said some hurtful things—I called her a child, she called me a crappy best friend, but it wasn't like we'd never had a fight before. Best friends fought.

When I got home from Cousins, I put Taylor's shoes and her clothes in a bag, ready to take them over to her house as soon as she gave me the signal that we were done being mad at each other. It was always Taylor who gave the signal, she was the one who initiated making up.

I waited, but it didn't come. I went to Marcy's a couple of times, hoping I'd run into her and we'd be forced to talk things out. Those times I was at Marcy's, she never came. Weeks passed. The summer was almost over.

Jeremiah kept saying the same thing he'd been saying for all of July and most of August. "Don't worry, you guys will make up. You guys always make up."

"You don't get it, this isn't like before," I told him. "She wouldn't even look at me."

"All of this over a party," he said, which pissed me off.

"It's not over a party."

"I know, I know—hold on a sec, Bells." I heard him talking to someone, and then he came back on the phone. "Our hot wings just got here. Want me to call you back after I eat? I can be quick."

"No, that's all right," I said.

"Don't be mad."

I said, "I'm not," and I wasn't. Not really. How could he understand what was going on with me and Taylor? He was a guy. He didn't get it. He didn't get how important, how really and truly vital, it was to me that Taylor and I start off our last year of high school together by each other's side.

So why couldn't I just call her, then? It was partly pride and partly something else. I was the one who had been pulling away from her this whole time, she was the one who had been holding on. Maybe I thought I was growing past her, maybe it was all for the best. We'd have to say good-bye next fall, maybe it would be easier this way. Maybe we'd been codependent, maybe more me on her than the other way around, and now I needed to stand on my own feet. This is what I told myself.

When I told this to Jeremiah the next night, he said, "Just call her."

I was pretty sure he was just sick of hearing me talk about it, so I said, "Maybe. I'll think about it."

The week before school started, the week I usually came back from Cousins, we always went back-to-school shopping together. Always. We'd been doing it since elementary school. She always knew the right kind of jeans to get. We'd go to Bath & Body Works and get those "Buy Three, Get One Free" kind of deals, and then we'd come home and split everything up so we each had a lotion, a body gel, a scrub. We'd be set until Christmas, at least.

That year, I went with my mom. My mom hated shopping. We were waiting in line to pay for jeans when Taylor and her mom walked into the store carrying a couple of shopping bags each. "Luce!" my mom called out.

Mrs. Jewel waved and came right over, with Taylor trailing behind her wearing sunglasses and cutoff shorts. My mom hugged Taylor, and Mrs. Jewel hugged me and said, "It's been a long time, honey."

To my mom, she said, "Laurel, can you believe our little girls are all grown up now? My gosh, I remember when they insisted on doing everything together. Baths, haircuts, everything."

"I remember," my mother said, smiling.

I caught Taylor's eye. Our moms kept on talking, and we just stood there looking at each other but not really.

After a minute, Taylor pulled out her cell phone. I didn't want to let this moment pass without saying something to her. I asked, "Did you get anything good?"

She nodded. Since she was wearing sunglasses, it was hard to tell what she was thinking. But I knew Taylor well. She loved to brag about her bargains.

Taylor hesitated and then said, "I got some hot boots for twenty-five percent off. And a couple of sundresses that I can winterize with tights and sweaters."

I nodded. Then it was our turn to pay, and I said, "Well, see you at school."

"See you," she said, turning away.

Without thinking, I handed the jeans to my mom and stopped Taylor. It could be the last time we ever talked to each other if I didn't say something. "Wait," I said. "Do you want to come over tonight? I bought a new skirt, but I don't know if I should tuck shirts into it or what . . ."

She pursed her lips for a second and then said, "Okay. Call me."

Taylor did come over that night. She showed me how to wear the skirt—which shoes looked best with it and which tops. Things weren't the same with us, not right away, and maybe not ever. We were growing up. We were still figuring out how to be in each other's lives without being everything to each other.

The truly ironic thing is that we ended up at the same school. Of all the schools in all the world, we ended up at each other's. It was fated. We were meant to be friends. We were meant to be in each other's lives, and you know what? I welcomed it. We weren't together all the time like we used to be—she had her sorority friends, I had my friends from my hall. But we still had each other.

chapter *eleven*

The next day, I couldn't hold out any longer. I called Jeremiah. I told him I needed to see him, that he should come over, and my voice shook as I said it. Over the phone, I could hear how grateful he was, how eager to make amends. I tried to justify calling him so fast by telling myself that I needed to see him face-to-face in order to move on. The truth was, I missed him. I, probably just as much as he did, wanted to figure out a way to forget what had happened.

But as much as I'd missed him, when I opened my door and saw his face again, all the hurt came rushing back, hard and fast. Jeremiah could see it too. At first he looked hopeful, and then he just looked devastated. When he tried to pull me to him, I wanted to hug him, but I couldn't let myself. Instead I shook my head and pushed him away from me.

We sat on my bed, our backs against the wall, our legs hanging off the edge.

I said, "How would I know that you wouldn't do it again? How would I be able to trust that?"

He got up. For a second I thought he was leaving, and my heart nearly stopped.

But then he got down on one knee, right in front of me. Very softly, he said, "You could marry me."

At first I wasn't sure I'd heard him right. But then he said it again, this time louder. "Marry me."

He reached into his jeans pocket and pulled out a ring. A silver ring with a little diamond in the center. "This would just be for starters, until I could afford to pay for a ring myself—with my money, not my dad's."

I couldn't feel my body. He was still talking, and I couldn't even hear. All I could do was stare at the ring in his hand.

"I love you so much. These past couple of days have been hell for me without you." He took a breath. "I'm so sorry for hurting you, Bells. What I did—was unforgivable. I know that I hurt us, that I'm going to have to work really hard to get you to trust me again. I'll do whatever it takes if you'll let me. Would you . . . be willing to let me try?"

"I don't know," I whispered.

He swallowed, and his Adam's apple bobbed up and down. "I'll try so hard, I swear to you. We'll get an apartment off campus, we can fix it up nice. I'll do the laundry. I'll learn how to cook stuff other than ramen and cereal."

"Putting cereal in a bowl isn't really cooking," I said, looking away from him because this picture he was putting in my head, it was too much. I could see it too. How sweet it could be. The two of us, just starting out, in our own place.

Jeremiah grabbed my hands, and I snatched them away from him. He said, "Don't you see, Belly? It's been our story all along. Yours and mine. Nobody else's."

I closed my eyes, trying to clear my head. Opening them, I said, "You just want to erase what you did by marrying me."

"No. That's not what this is. What happened the other night"—he hesitated—"it made me realize something. I don't ever want to be without you. Ever. You are the only girl for me. I've always known it. In this whole world, I will never love another girl the way I love you."

He took my hand again, and this time I didn't pull away from him. "Do you still love me?" he asked.

I swallowed. "Yeah."

"Then please, marry me."

I said, "You can't ever hurt me like that again." It was half warning, half plea.

"I won't," he said, and I knew he meant it.

He looked at me so determinedly, so earnestly. I knew his face well, maybe better than anybody now. Every line, every curve. The little bump on his nose from when he broke it surfing, the almost-faded scar on his forehead from the time he and Conrad were wrestling in the rec room and they knocked a plant over. I was there for those moments. Maybe I knew his face even better than my own—the hours I'd spent staring at it while he slept, tracing my finger along his cheekbone. Maybe he'd done the same things to me.

I didn't want to see a mark on his face one day and not know how it got there. I wanted to be with him. His was the face I loved.

Wordlessly, I slipped my left hand out of his, and Jeremiah's face slackened. Then I held out my hand for him, and his eyes lit up. The joy I felt in that moment— I couldn't even put it into words. His hand shook as he placed the ring on my finger.

He asked, "Isabel Conklin, will you marry me?" in as serious a voice as I'd ever heard him use.

"Yes, I'll marry you," I said.

He put his arms around me, and we held on to each other, clinging like we were the other's safe harbor. All I could think was, if we just get through this storm, we will make it. He'd made mistakes, I had too. But we loved each other, and that was what mattered.

We made plans all night—where we would live, how we would tell our parents. The past few days felt like another lifetime ago. That day, without another word about it, we decided to leave the past in the past. The future was where we were headed.

chapter *twelve*

That night I dreamed of Conrad. I was the same age I was now, but he was younger, ten or eleven maybe. I think he might even have been wearing overalls. We played outside my house until it got dark, just running around the yard. I said, "Susannah will be wondering where you are. You should go home." He said, "I can't. I don't know how. Will you help me?" And then I was sad, because I didn't know how either. We weren't at my house anymore, and it was so dark. We were in the woods. We were lost.

When I woke up, I was crying and Jeremiah was asleep next to me. I sat up in the bed. It was dark, the only light in the room was my alarm clock. It read 4:57. I lay back down.

I wiped my eyes, and then I breathed in Jeremiah's scent, the sweetness of his face, the way his chest rose and fell as he breathed. He was there. He was solid and real and next to me, crammed in close the way you have to be when you are sleeping in a dorm-room bed. We were that close now.

In the morning, when I woke up, I didn't remember right away. The dream was there in the back of my head, in a place I couldn't get to. It was fading fast, almost all the way, but not quite, not yet. I had to think hard and fast to piece it all together, to hold on to it.

I started to sit up, but Jeremiah pulled me back toward him and said, "Five more minutes." He was the big spoon, and I was the little spoon tucked into my spot in his arms. I closed my eyes, willing myself to remember before it was gone. Like those last few seconds before the sun sets—going, going, and then gone. Remember, remember, or the dream will slip away forever.

Jeremiah started to say something about breakfast, and I covered his mouth and said, "Shh. One sec."

And then I had it. Conrad, and how funny he looked in his denim overalls. The two of us playing outside for hours. I let out a sigh. I felt so relieved.

"What were you saying?" I asked Jeremiah.

"Breakfast," he said, planting a kiss on my palm.

Snuggling in closer to him, I said, "Five more minutes."

chapter *thirteen*

I wanted to tell everyone face-to-face, all at once. In a weird way, it would be perfect timing. Our families would be together in Cousins in a week. A battered-women's shelter that Susannah had volunteered at and fund-raised for had planted a garden in her honor, and there was going to be a little ceremony next Saturday. We were all going—me, Jere, my mom, his dad, Steven. Conrad.

I hadn't seen Conrad since Christmas. He was supposed to fly back for my mother's fiftieth birthday party, but he bailed at the last minute. "Typical Con," Jeremiah had said, shaking his head. He'd looked at me, waiting for me to agree. I didn't say anything.

My mother and Conrad had a special relationship, always had. They got each other on some level I didn't understand. After Susannah died, they became closer, maybe because they grieved for her in the same way—alone. My mom and Conrad spoke on the phone often, about what I didn't know. So when he didn't come, I could see how disappointed she was, even though she didn't say so. I wanted to tell her, Love him all you want, but don't expect anything in return. Conrad isn't someone who can be counted on.

He did send a nice bouquet of red zinnias, though. "My favorite," she'd said, beaming.

What would he say when we told him our news? I couldn't begin to guess. When it came to Conrad, I was never sure of anything.

I worried, too, about what my mother would say. Jeremiah wasn't worried, but he so rarely was. He said, "Once they know we're serious, they'll have to get on board, because they won't be able to stop us. We're adults now."

We were walking back from the dining hall. Jeremiah dropped my hand, jumped onto a bench, threw his head back, and yelled, "Hey, everybody! Belly Conklin is gonna marry me!"

A few people turned to look but then kept walking.

"Get down from there," I said, laughing and covering my face with my hoodie.

He jumped back down and ran around the bench once, his arms up and out like an airplane. He zoomed back over to me and lifted me up by the armpits. "Come on, fly," he encouraged.

I rolled my eyes and moved my arms up and down. "Happy?"

"Yes," he said, setting me back down on the ground.

I was too. *This* was the Jere I knew. This was the boy from the beach house. Getting engaged, promising to be each other's forever, it made me feel like even with all the changes over the past few years, he was still the same boy and I was still the same girl. Now nobody could take that away from us, not anymore.

chapter *fourteen*

I knew I had to talk to Taylor and Anika before my dad
came and got me in the morning. I debated just telling
them together, but I knew that Taylor would be hurt if
I lumped her, my oldest friend, with Anika, who I had
known for less than a year. I had to tell Taylor first. I
owed her that much.

I knew she'd think we were crazy. Getting back
together was one thing, but getting married was something else entirely. Unlike most of her sorority sisters,
Taylor didn't want to get married until she was at least
twenty-eight.

I called and asked her to meet me at the Drip House,
the coffee shop everyone studied at. I told her I had news.
She tried to get it out of me over the phone, but I resisted,
saying, "It's the kind of news you have to tell in person."

Taylor was already seated with her nonfat iced latte when I got there. She had on her Ray-Bans, and she was texting. She put down her phone when she saw me.

I sat down across from her, careful to keep my hand in my lap.

Taking off her sunglasses, she said, "You're looking much better today."

"Thanks, Tay. I feel a lot better."

"So what's up?" She scrutinized me. "Did you guys get back together? Or did you break up for real?"

I held up my left hand with a flourish. She looked at it, confused. Then her eyes focused on my ring finger.

Taylor's eyes turned huge. "You're effing kidding me. You're engaged?!" she screamed. A couple of people turned around and looked at us, annoyed. I shrank down in my seat a little. Grabbing my hand, she said, "Oh my God! Let me see that thing!"

I could tell she thought it was too small, but I didn't care.

"Oh my God," she said, still staring at the ring.

"I know," I said.

"But, Belly . . . he cheated on you."

"We're starting over fresh. I really love him, Tay."

"Yeah, but the timing is kinda suspect," she said slowly. "I mean, it's really sudden."

"It is and it isn't. You said it yourself. This is Jere we're talking about. He's the love of my life."

She just stared at me, her mouth an O. She sputtered, "But—but why can't you wait at least until after you finish college?"

"We don't see the point in waiting if we're gonna get married anyways." I took a sip of Taylor's drink. "We're gonna get an apartment. You can help me pick out curtains and stuff."

"I guess," she said. "But wait, what about your mom? Did Laurel flip her shit?"

"We're telling my mom and his dad next week in Cousins. We'll tell my dad after."

She perked up. "Wait, so nobody even knows yet? Just me?"

I nodded, and I could tell Taylor was pleased. She loves being in on a secret—it's one of her top favorite things in life.

"It's gonna be an apocalypse," she said, taking her drink back. "Like, dead bodies. Like, blood in the streets. And when I say blood, I mean your blood."

"Gee, thanks a lot, Tay."

"I'm just speaking the truth. Laurel is the OG feminist. She's like Gloria freaking Steinem. She's not gonna like this one bit. She'll go all Terminator on his ass. And yours."

"My mom loves Jeremiah. She and Susannah always talked about me marrying one of her sons. It might be, like, a dream come true for her. In fact, I bet it will be." I knew that wasn't the least bit true even as I was saying it.

Taylor looked unconvinced too. "Maybe," she said. "So when is this happening?"

"This August."

"That's really, really soon. Hardly gives us any time to plan." Chewing on her straw, she cast a sneaky look my way. "What about bridesmaids? Are you going to have a maid of honor?"

"I don't know. . . . We want it to be really small. We're gonna do it at the Cousins house. Really casual, like, not a big deal."

"Not a big deal? You're getting married and you don't want it to be a big deal?"

"I didn't mean it like that. I just don't care about all that stuff. All I want is to be with Jeremiah."

"All what stuff?"

"Like, bridesmaids and wedding cake. Stuff like that."

"Liar!" She pointed her finger at me. "You wanted five bridesmaids and a four-tier carrot cake. You wanted an ice sculpture of a human heart with your initials carved into it. Which, by the way, is gross."

"Tay!"

She held up her hand to stop me. "You wanted a live band and crab cakes and a balloon drop after your first dance. What was that song you wanted to dance to?"

"'Stay' by Maurice Williams and the Zodiacs," I said automatically. "But Taylor, I was probably ten years old when I said all that stuff." I was really touched that she remembered, though. But I guessed I remembered everything Taylor wanted too. Doves, little lace gloves, hot-pink stiletto heels.

"You should have everything you want, Belly," Taylor said, her chin jutting out in her stubborn Taylor way. "You only get married once."

"I know, but we don't have the money. And anyway, I don't really care about those things anymore. That was kid stuff." But maybe I didn't have to do *all* of it, maybe just some of it. Maybe I could still have a real wedding, but simple. Because, it would be nice to wear a wedding dress and to have a father-daughter dance with my dad.

"I thought Jeremy's dad was loaded. Can't he afford to give you a real wedding?"

"There's no way my mom would let him pay for it. Besides, like I said, we don't want anything fancy."

"Okay," she conceded. "We'll forget the ice sculpture. But balloons are cheap—we can still do balloons. And the carrot cake. We could just do a regular two-layer, I guess. And I don't care what you say, you're wearing a wedding dress."

"That sounds good," I agreed, taking a sip of her drink. It felt really nice to have Taylor's blessing. It was like getting permission to be excited, something I didn't know I needed or wanted.

"And you'll still have bridesmaids. Or at least a maid of honor."

"I'll just have you."

Taylor looked pleased. "But what about Anika? You don't want Anika to be a bridesmaid?"

"Hmm, maybe," I said, and when her face fell, just slightly, I added, "But I want you to be my maid of honor. Okay?"

Tears filled her eyes. "I'm so honored."

Taylor Jewel, my oldest friend in the world. We'd been through some times together, and I knew now it was pure grace that we'd managed to come out the other side.

chapter *fifteen*

Anika was next, and I was dreading it. I respected her opinion. I didn't want her to think less of me. The prospect of being a bridesmaid wasn't going to have any sway over her. That wasn't something she would care about either way.

We had decided to room together that fall, in a suite with two of our other friends, Shay and Lynn, in the new dorm on the other side of campus. Anika and I were going to buy cute plates and cups, she was bringing her fridge, and I was bringing my TV. Everything was set.

We were hanging out in her room later that night. I was packing her books inside a big crate, and she was rolling up her posters.

The radio was on, and our campus station was playing Madonna's "The Power of Good-Bye." Maybe it was a sign.

I sat on the floor, putting away the last book, trying to

drum up the courage to tell her. Nervously, I licked my lips. "Ani, I have something I need to talk to you about," I said.

She'd been struggling with the movie poster on the back of her door. "What's up?"

There's no greater power than the power of good-bye.

I swallowed. "I feel really bad having to do this to you."

Anika turned around. "Do what?"

"I'm not going to be able to room with you next semester."

Her eyebrows were knit together. "What? Why? Did something happen?"

"Jeremiah asked me to marry him."

She did a double take. "Isabel Conklin! Shut the shit up."

Slowly, I held up my hand.

Anika whistled. "Wow. That's crazy."

"I know."

She opened her mouth, then closed it. Then she said, "Do you know what you're doing?"

"Yeah. I think so. I really, really love him."

"Where are you guys going to live?"

"In an apartment off campus." I hesitated. "I just feel bad about letting you down. Are you mad?"

Shaking her head, she said, "I'm not mad. I mean, yeah, it sucks that we won't be living together, but I'll figure something out. I could ask Trina from my dance team. Or my cousin Brandy might be transferring here. She could be our fourth."

So it wasn't such a big deal after all, my not living with them. Life goes on, I guessed. I felt a little wistful, imagining what it would be like if I was still the fourth. Shay was really good at doing hair, and Lynn loved to bake cupcakes. It would have been fun.

Anika sat down on her bed. "I'll be fine. I'm just . . . surprised."

"Me too."

When she didn't say anything else, I asked, "Do you think I'm making a huge mistake?"

In her thoughtful way, she asked, "Does it matter what I think?"

"Yes."

"It's not for me to judge, Iz."

"But you're my friend. I respect your opinion. I don't want you to think badly of me."

"You care too much about what other people think." She said it with sureness but also tenderness.

If anyone else had said it—my mother, Taylor, even Jere—I would have bristled. But not with Anika. With her, I couldn't really mind. In a way it was flattering to have her see me so clearly and still like me. Friendship in college was different that way. You spend all this time with people, sometimes every day, every meal. There was no hiding who you were in front of your friends. You were just naked. Especially in front of someone like Anika, who was so frank and open and incisive and said whatever she thought. She didn't miss a thing.

Anika said, "At least you'll never have to wear shower shoes again."

"Or have to pull other people's hair out of the drain," I added. "Jeremiah's hair is too short to get caught."

"You'll never have to hide your food." Anika's roommate, Joy, was always stealing her food, and Anika had taken to hiding granola bars in her underwear drawer.

"I might actually have to do that. Jere eats a lot," I said, twisting my ring around my finger.

I stayed a while longer, helping her take down the rest of her posters, collecting the dust bunnies under her bed with an old sock I used as a mitten. We talked about the magazine internship Anika had lined up for the summer, and me maybe going to visit her in New York for a weekend.

After, I walked down the hall back to my room. For the first time all year, it was really quiet—no hair dryers going, no one sitting in the hallway on the phone, no one microwaving popcorn in the commons area. A lot of people had already gone home for the summer. Tomorrow I would be gone too.

College life as I knew it was about to change.

chapter *sixteen*

I didn't plan to start going by Isabel. It just happened. All my life, everyone had called me Belly and I didn't really have a say in it. For the first time in a long time, I did have a say, but it didn't occur to me until we—Jeremiah, my mom, my dad, and me—were standing in front of my dorm room door on freshman move-in day. My dad and Jeremiah were lugging the TV, my mom had a suitcase, and I was carrying a laundry basket with all my toiletries and picture frames. Sweat was pouring down my dad's back, and his maroon button-down shirt had three wet spots. Jeremiah was sweating too, since he'd been trying to impress my dad all morning by insisting on bringing up the heaviest stuff. It made my dad feel awkward, I could tell.

"Hurry, Belly," my dad said, breathing hard.

"She's Isabel now," my mother said.

I remember the way I fumbled with my key and how I looked up at the door and saw it. ISABEL, it said in glue-on rhinestones. My roommate's and my door tags were made out of empty CD cases. My roommate's, Jillian Capel's, was a Mariah Carey CD, and mine was Prince.

Jillian's stuff was already unpacked, on the left side of the room, closer to the door. She had a paisley bedspread, navy and rusty orange. It looked brand new. She'd already hung up her posters—a *Trainspotting* movie poster and some band I'd never heard of called Running Water.

My dad sat down at the empty desk—my desk. He pulled out a handkerchief and wiped off his forehead. He looked really tired. "It's a good room," he said. "Good light."

Jeremiah was just hovering around, and he said, "I'll go down to the car to get that big box."

My dad started to get up. "I'll help," he said.

"I've got it," Jeremiah said, bounding out the door.

Sitting back down, my dad looked relieved. "I'll just take a break, then," he said.

Meanwhile, my mother was surveying the room, opening the closet, looking in drawers.

I sank down on the bed. So this was where I was going to live for the next year. Next door, someone was playing jazz. Down the hall, I could hear a girl arguing with her mother about where to put her laundry bin. It seemed like the elevator never stopped dinging open and closed. I didn't mind. I liked the noise. It was comforting knowing there were people all around me.

"Want me to unpack your clothes?" my mother asked.

"No, that's all right," I said. I wanted to do that myself. Then it would really feel like my room.

"At least let me make up your bed, then," she said.

When it was time to say good-bye, I wasn't ready. I thought I would be, but I wasn't. My dad stood there, his hands on his hips. His hair looked really gray in the light. He said, "Well, we should get going if we want to beat rush-hour traffic."

Irritably, my mother said, "We'll be fine."

Seeing them together like this, it was almost like they weren't divorced, like we were still a family. I was overcome with this sudden rush of thankfulness. Not all divorces were like theirs. For Steven's and my sake, they made it work and they were sincere about it. There was still genuine affection between them, but more than that: there was love for us. It was what made it possible for them to come together on days like this.

I hugged my dad, and I was surprised to see tears in his eyes. He never cried. My mother hugged me briskly, but I knew it was because she didn't want to let go. "Make sure you wash your sheets at least twice a month," she said.

"Okay," I said.

"And try making your bed in the morning. It'll make your room look nicer."

"Okay," I said again.

My mother looked over at the other side of the room. "I just wish we could have met your roommate."

Jeremiah was sitting at my desk, his head down, scrolling on his phone while we said our good-byes.

All of a sudden, my dad said, "Jeremiah, are you going to leave now too?"

Startled, Jeremiah looked up. "Oh, I was going to take Belly to dinner."

My mother shot me a look, and I knew what she was thinking. A couple of nights before, she'd given me this long speech about meeting new people and not spending all my time with Jere. Girls with boyfriends, she'd said, limit themselves to a certain kind of college experience. I'd promised her I wouldn't be one of those kind of girls.

"Just don't get her back too late," my dad said in this really meaningful kind of way.

I could feel my cheeks get red, and this time my mother gave my dad a look, which made me feel even more awkward. But Jeremiah just said, "Oh, yeah, of course," in his relaxed way.

I met my roommate, Jillian, later that night, after dinner. It was in the elevator, right after Jeremiah dropped me off in front of the dorm. I recognized her right away, from the pictures on her dresser. She had curly brown hair, and she was really little, shorter than she'd looked in the pictures.

I stood there, trying to figure out what to say. When the other girls in the elevator got off on the sixth floor, it was just the two of us. I cleared my throat and said, "Excuse me. Are you Jillian Capel?"

"Yeah," she said, and I could tell she was a little weirded out.

"I'm Isabel Conklin," I said. "Your roommate."

I wondered if I should hug her or offer her my hand to shake. I did neither, because she was staring at me.

"Oh, hi. How are you?" Without waiting for me to answer, she said, "I'm just coming back from dinner with my parents." Later, I would learn that she said "How are you" a lot, like it was more of a thing to say, not something she expected an answer to.

"I'm good," I said. "I just had dinner too."

We got off the elevator then. I felt this excited pitter-patter in my chest, like wow, this is my roommate. This was the person I was going to be living with for a whole year. I'd thought a lot about her since I got my housing letter. Jillian Capel from Washington, DC, nonsmoker. I'd imagined us talking all night, sharing secrets and shoes and microwave popcorn.

When we were in our room, Jillian sat down on her bed and said, "Do you have a boyfriend?"

"Yeah, he goes here too," I said, sitting on my hands. I was eager to get right to the girl talk and the bonding. "His name is Jeremiah. He's a sophomore."

I jumped up and grabbed a photo of us from my desk. It was from graduation, and Jeremiah was wearing a tie and he looked handsome in it. Shyly, I handed it to her.

"He's really cute," she said.

"Thanks. Do you have a boyfriend?"

She nodded. "Back home."

"Neat," I said, because it was all I could think of. "What's his name?"

"Simon."

When she didn't elaborate, I asked, "So, do people ever call you Jill? Or Jilly? Or do you just go by Jillian?"

"Jillian. Do you go to sleep early or late?"

"Late. What about you?"

"Early," she said, chewing on her lower lip. "We'll figure something out. I wake up early, too. What about you?"

"Um, sure, sometimes." I hated to wake up early, hated it more than almost anything.

"Do you like to study with music on or off?"

"Off?"

Jillian looked relieved. "Oh, good. I hate noise when I study. I need it to be really quiet." She added, "Not that I'm anal or anything."

I nodded. Her picture frames were at perfect right angles. When we walked into the room, she'd hung up her jean jacket right away. I only ever made my bed when company came over. I wondered if my sloppy tendencies would get on her nerves. I hoped not.

I was about to say so when she turned her laptop on. I guessed we were done bonding for the night. Now that my parents were gone and Jeremiah was on his way back to his frat house, I was really alone. I didn't know what to do with myself. I'd already unpacked. I'd been hoping we could explore the hall together, meet people. But she was typing away, chatting with someone. Probably her boyfriend back home.

I got my cell phone out of my purse and texted Jeremiah. *Will you come back?*

I knew he would.

For the hall icebreaker the next night, our RA, Kira, told us to bring one personal item that we felt represented us best. I settled on a pair of swim goggles. The other girls brought stuffed animals and framed photos, and one girl brought out her modeling book. Jillian brought her laptop.

We were all sitting in a circle, and Joy was sitting across from me. She was cradling a trophy in her lap. It was for a soccer state championship, which I thought was pretty impressive. I really wanted to make friends with Joy. I'd had it in my head since the night before, when we'd chatted in the hall bathroom in our pajamas, both of us with our shower caddies. Joy was short, with a sandy bob and light eyes. She didn't wear makeup. She was sturdy and sure of herself, in the way that girls who play competitive sports are.

"I'm Joy," she said. "My team won the state championship. If any of you guys like soccer, hit me up and we'll get a hall league going."

When it was my turn, I said, "I'm Isabel. I like to swim," and Joy smiled at me.

I always thought that college would be It. Like, instant friends, a place to belong. I didn't think it would be this hard.

I'd thought there would be parties and mixers and midnight runs to the Waffle House. I'd been at college for four whole days, and I hadn't done any of those things. Jillian and I had eaten in the dining hall together, but that was about it. She was mostly on the phone with her boyfriend or on the computer. There had been no mention of clubbing or frat parties. I had a feeling Jillian was above that kind of thing.

I wasn't, and Taylor wasn't either. I'd gone to visit her dorm once already, and she and her roommate were like two peas in a trendy little color-coordinated pod. Her roommate's boyfriend was in a fraternity, and he lived off campus. Taylor said she'd call if there were any cool parties that weekend, but so far, she hadn't. Taylor was taking to college like a goldfish to its brand-new tank, and I just wasn't. I'd told Jeremiah I'd be busy making friends and bonding with my roommate so I probably wouldn't see him until the weekend. I didn't want to go back on that. I didn't want to be one of those girls.

Thursday night that first week, a bunch of girls were drinking in Joy's room. I could hear them down the hallway. I had been filling out my new planner, writing in all my classes and things. Jillian was at the library. We'd only had one day of classes so far, so I didn't know what she could possibly be studying. I still wished she'd asked me to go with her, though. Jeremiah had asked if I wanted him to come pick me up, but I'd said no, in the hopes that I would be invited somewhere. So far, it was just me and the planner.

But then Joy popped her head in my doorway, which I'd been keeping open the same way the other girls had. "Isabel, come and hang with us," she said.

"Sure!" I said, practically leaping out of my bed. I felt this surge of hope and excitement. Maybe these were my people.

There was Joy, her roommate Anika, Molly, who lived at the end the hall, and Shay, the girl with the modeling book. They were all sitting on the floor, a big bottle of Gatorade in the middle, only, it didn't look like Gatorade. It was light brownish yellow— Tequila, I guessed. I hadn't touched tequila since I'd gotten drunk off of it in Cousins the summer before.

"Come sit down," Joy said, patting the floor next to her. "We're playing I Never. Have you ever played before?"

"No," I said, sitting down next to her.

"Basically, when it's your turn, you say something

like, 'I never . . .'"—Anika looked around the circle—"hooked up with someone related to me."

Everyone giggled. "And if you have, you have to drink," Molly finished, chewing on her thumbnail.

"I'll start," said Joy, leaning forward. "I never . . . cheated on a test."

Shay grabbed the bottle and took a swig. "What? I was busy modeling, I didn't have time to study," she said, and everyone laughed again.

Molly went next. "I never did it with anyone in public!"

That time, Joy took the bottle. "It was at a park," she explained. "It was getting dark. I doubt anyone saw us."

Shay said, "Does a restaurant bathroom count?"

I could feel my face get hot. I was dreading my turn. I hadn't done much of anything. My I Nevers could probably last all night.

"I never hooked up with Chad from the fourth floor!" Molly said, collapsing into a fit of giggles.

Joy threw a pillow at her. "No fair! I told you that in secret."

"Drink! Drink!" everyone chanted.

Joy took a swig. Wiping her mouth, she said, "Your turn, Isabel."

My mouth felt dry all of a sudden. "I never . . ." Had sex. "I never . . . played this game before," I finished lamely.

I could feel Joy's disappointment in me. Maybe she'd

thought we could be close friends too and now she was rethinking it.

Anika chuckled just to be polite, and then they all took turns drinking before Joy started it up again with, "I never went skinny-dipping in the ocean. In a pool, though!"

Nope, never did that either. Almost, that time I was fifteen, with Cam Cameron. But almost didn't count.

I ended up taking one drink when Molly said, "I never dated two people in the same family."

"You dated brothers?" Joy asked me, looking interested all of a sudden. "Or a brother and a sister?"

Coughing a little, I said, "Brothers."

"Twins?" Shay said.

"At the same time?" Molly wanted to know.

"No, not at the same time. And they're just regular brothers," I said. "They're a year apart."

"That's kind of badass," Joy said, giving me an approving look.

And then we went on to the next thing. When Shay said she'd never stolen before and Joy took a drink, I saw the look on Anika's face, and I had to bite the insides of my cheeks to keep from laughing. She saw me, and we exchanged a secret look.

I saw Joy around after that, in the hall bathroom and in the study, and we talked, but we never became close. Jillian and I never became best buddies either, but she ended up being a pretty good roommate.

Of all those girls, Anika was the one I ended up being closest to. Even though we were the same age, she took me under her wing like a little sister, and for once I didn't mind being the little sister. Anika was too cool for me to care. She smelled the way I imagined wildflowers smelled when they grew in sand. Later, I found out it was the oil she put in her hair. Anika almost never gossiped, she didn't eat meat, and she was a dancer. I admired all of those things about her.

I was sorry we'd never be roommates. From now on, I'd only ever have one roommate again—Jeremiah, my soon-to-be husband.

chapter *seventeen*

I woke up early the next day. I showered, threw away my shower shoes, and got ready one last time in my dorm room. I didn't put my ring on, just in case. I put it in the zippered pocket in my purse. My dad wasn't the most observant guy when it came to accessories, so it wasn't likely he'd notice, but still.

My dad was at the dorm by ten o'clock to move me out. Jeremiah helped. I didn't even have to give him a wakeup call the way I'd planned; he showed up at my room at nine thirty with coffee and donuts for my dad.

I stopped in some of the girls' rooms, hugging them good-bye, wishing them good summers. Lorrie said, "See you in August," and Jules said, "We have to hang out more next year." I said good-bye to Anika last, and I teared up a little. She hugged me and said, "Chill out. I'll see you at the wedding. Tell Taylor I'll be e-mailing her about our bridesmaid dresses." I laughed out loud. Taylor was going to love that. Not.

After we were done loading up the car, my dad took us to lunch at a steak restaurant. It wasn't super fancy, but it was nice, a family place with leather booths and pickles at the table.

"Order whatever you like, guys," my dad said, sliding into the booth.

Jeremiah and I sat across from him. I looked at the menu and picked the New York strip because it was cheapest. My dad wasn't poor, but he definitely wasn't rich, either.

When the waitress came over to take our orders, my dad ordered the salmon, I got the New York strip, and Jeremiah said, "I'll have the dry-aged rib eye, medium rare."

The rib eye was the most expensive thing on the menu. It cost thirty-eight dollars. I looked at him and thought, he probably didn't even look at the price. He never had to, not when all his bills got sent to his dad. Things were gonna change when we were married, that was for sure. No more spending money on dumb stuff like vintage Air Jordans or steak.

"So, what do you have going on this summer, Jeremiah?" my dad asked.

Jeremiah looked at me and then back at my dad and

then back at me. I shook my head just slightly. I had this vision of him asking my dad for his blessing, and it was all wrong. My dad couldn't find out before my mother.

"I'm going to be interning at my dad's company again," Jeremiah said.

"Good for you," my dad said. "That'll keep you busy."

"For sure."

My dad looked at me. "What about you, Belly? Are you going to waitress again?"

I sucked soda from the bottom of my glass. "Yeah. I'm gonna go in and talk to my old manager next week. They always need help in the summer, so it should be all right."

With the wedding just a couple of months away, I would just have to work doubly—triply—hard.

When the bill came, I saw my dad squint and take a closer look. I hoped Jeremiah didn't notice, but when I realized he hadn't, I kind of wished he had.

I always felt closest to my dad when I was sitting in the passenger seat of his minivan, studying his profile, the two us listening to his Bill Evans CD. Drives with my dad were our quiet times together, when we might talk about nothing and everything.

So far the drive had been a quiet one.

He was humming along with the music when I said, "Dad?"

"Hmm?"

I wanted to tell him so badly. I wanted to share it with him, to have it happen during this perfect moment when I was still his little girl in the passenger seat and he was still the one driving the car. It would be a moment just between us. I'd stopped calling him Daddy in middle school, but it was in my heart—Daddy, I'm getting married.

"Nothing," I said at last.

I couldn't do it. I couldn't tell him before I told my mother. It wouldn't be right.

He went back to humming.

Just a little bit longer, Dad.

chapter *eighteen*

I'd thought it would take at least a little time to adjust to being at home again after being away at college, but I fell back into my old routine pretty much right away. Before the end of the first week, I was unpacked and having early-morning breakfasts with my mom and fighting with my brother Steven over the state of the bathroom we shared. I was messy, but Steven took it to a whole new level. I guessed it ran in our family. And I started working at Behrs again, taking as many shifts as they would let me, sometimes two a day.

The night before we all went to Cousins for the dedication of Susannah's garden, Jere and I were talking on the phone. We were talking about wedding stuff, and I told him some of Taylor's ideas. He loved them all but balked at the idea of a carrot cake.

"I want a chocolate cake," he said. "With raspberry filling."

"Maybe one layer can be carrot and one can be chocolate," I suggested, cradling the phone to my shoulder. "I've heard they can do that."

I was sitting on my bedroom floor, counting my tips for the night. I hadn't even changed out of my work shirt yet, even though it had grease stains all down the front, but I was too beat to bother. I just loosened the necktie.

"A chocolate-raspberry-carrot cake?"

"With cream cheese frosting for my layer," I reminded him.

"Sounds kinda complicated to me flavor profilewise, but fine. Let's do it."

I smiled to myself as I stacked my ones and fives and tens. Jeremiah was watching a lot of Food Network since he'd been home.

"Well, first we have to be able to pay for this alleged cake," I said. "I've been taking all the shifts I can, and I've only got a hundred and twenty bucks saved so far. Taylor says wedding cakes are really expensive. Maybe I should ask her mom to bake the cake instead. Mrs. Jewel's a really good baker. We probably couldn't ask for anything too fancy, though."

Jeremiah had been silent on the other line. Then he finally said, "I don't know if you should keep working at Behrs."

"What are you talking about? We need the money."

"Yeah, but I have the money my mom left me. We can use that for the wedding. I don't like you having to work so hard."

"But you're working too!"

"I'm an intern. It's a bullshit job. I'm not working half as hard as you are for this wedding. I sit around an office, and you're busting your ass working double shifts at Behrs. It doesn't feel right."

"If this is because I'm the girl and you're the guy . . . ," I began.

"That's not it, dude. I'm just saying, why should you have to work this hard when I have money in my savings account?"

"I thought we said we were going to do this on our own."

"I've been doing some Internet research, and it looks like it's going to be a lot more expensive than we thought. Even if we go really simple, we still have to pay for food and drinks and flowers. We're only getting married once, Belly."

"True."

"My mom would want to contribute. Right?"

"I guess. . . ." Susannah would want to do more than contribute. She'd want to be there every step of the way—dress shopping, deciding on the flowers and food, all of it. She'd want to do it up. I always pictured her there on my wedding day, sitting next to my mom, wearing a fancy hat. It was a really nice picture.

"So let's let her contribute. Besides, you're gonna get really busy with wedding-planning stuff with Taylor. I'll help as much as I can, but I still have to be at work from nine to five. When you call caterers and flower people or whatever, that'll have to be during the day, and I won't be able to be there."

I was really impressed that he'd thought of all this. I liked this other side of him, thinking ahead, worrying about my health. I had just been complaining about calluses on my feet too.

"Let's talk more about it after we tell our parents," I told him.

"Are you still nervous?"

I'd been trying not to think about it too much. At Behrs, I focused all my energy on delivering bread baskets and refilling drinks and cutting slices of cheesecake. In a way, I was glad to be working double shifts, because it kept me out of the house and away from my mother's watchful eye. I hadn't worn my engagement ring since I'd been home. I only pulled it out at night, in my room.

I said, "I'm scared, but I'll be relieved to finally have it out in the open. I hate keeping things from my mom."

"I know," he said.

I looked at the clock. It was twelve thirty. "We're gonna leave early tomorrow morning, so I should probably go to sleep." I hesitated before asking, "Are you driving up with just your dad? What's the deal with Conrad?"

"I have no clue. I haven't talked to him. I think he's flying in tomorrow. We'll see if he even shows."

I wasn't sure if it was disappointment I was feeling or relief. Probably both. "I doubt he'll come," I said.

"You never know with Con. He might come, he might not." He added, "Don't forget to bring your ring."

"I won't."

Then we said good night, and it was a long time before I could fall asleep. I think I was afraid. Afraid that he was coming and afraid that he wasn't.

chapter *nineteen*

I was up before the alarm; I was showered with my new dress on before Steven was even awake. I was the first one in the car.

My dress was lavender silk chiffon. It had a tight bodice and narrow straps and a floaty skirt, the kind you'd spin around in like a girl in a musical. Something Kim MacAfee might wear. I'd seen it in a store window in February, when it was still too cold to wear it without tights. Tights would ruin it. I'd used my father's for-emergencies-only card, the one I'd never used before. The dress had stayed in my closet all this time, still covered in plastic.

When my mother saw me, she burst into a smile and said, "You look beautiful. Beck would love this dress."

Steven said, "Not bad," and I gave them both a little curtsy. It was just that kind of dress.

My mother drove, and I sat in front. Steven slept in the backseat, his mouth open. He was wearing a button-down shirt and khaki pants. My mother looked nice too in her navy pantsuit and cream pumps.

"Conrad's definitely coming today, right, bean?" my mother asked me.

"You're the one who talks to him, not me," I said. I put my bare feet on the dashboard. My high heels were in a heap on the floor of the car.

Checking her rearview mirror, my mother said, "I haven't spoken to Conrad in a few weeks, but I'm sure he'll be there. He wouldn't miss something as important as this."

When I didn't say anything, she glanced at me and said, "Do you disagree?"

"Sorry, Mom, but I wouldn't get my hopes up." I didn't know why I couldn't just agree with her. I didn't know what was holding me back.

Because I really did believe he was coming. If I didn't, would I have taken extra care with my hair that morning? In the shower, would I have shaved my legs not once but twice, just to be safe? Would I have put on that new dress and worn those heels that made my feet hurt if I truly didn't believe he was coming?

No. Deep down I more than believed it. I knew it.

"Have you heard anything from Conrad, Laurel?" Mr. Fisher asked my mother. We were standing in the parking lot of the women's center—Mr. Fisher, Jere, Steven, my mother, and me. People were starting to file into the building. Mr. Fisher had already checked inside twice: Conrad wasn't there.

My mother shook her head. "I haven't heard anything new. When I spoke to him last month, he said he was coming."

"If he's late, we can just save him a seat," I offered.

"I'd better get inside," Jeremiah said. He was accepting the plaque commemorating the day on behalf of Susannah.

We watched him go because there was nothing else to do. Then Mr. Fisher said, "Maybe we should go in too," and he looked defeated. I could see where he'd cut himself shaving. His chin looked raw.

"Let's do that," my mother said, straightening up. "Belly, why don't you wait here for another minute?"

"Sure," I said. "You guys go ahead. I'll wait."

When the three of them were inside, I sat down on the curb. My feet were hurting already. I waited for another ten minutes, and when he still didn't show, I got up. So he wasn't coming after all.

chapter *twenty*
CONRAD

I saw her before she saw me. In the front row, I saw her sitting with my dad and Laurel and Steven. She had her hair pulled back, pinned up on the sides. I'd never seen her wear her hair like that before. She had on a light purple dress. She looked grown up. It occurred to me that she had grown up while I wasn't looking, that there was every likelihood she had changed and I didn't know her anymore. But when she stood up to clap, I saw the Band-Aid on her ankle and I recognized her again. She was Belly. She kept messing with the barrettes in her hair. One was coming loose.

My plane had been delayed, and even though I'd done eighty the whole way to Cousins, I was still late. Jeremiah was starting his speech just as I walked in. There was an empty seat up front next to my dad, but I just stood in the back. I saw Laurel shift in her seat, scanning the room before turning back around. She didn't see me.

A woman from the shelter got up and thanked everyone for coming. She talked about how great my mom was, how dedicated she was to the shelter, how much money she raised for it, how much awareness in the community. She said my mom was a gift. It was funny, I'd known my mom was involved with the women's shelter, but I didn't know how much she gave of herself. I felt a jolt of shame as I remembered the time she'd asked me to go help her serve breakfast one Saturday morning. I'd blown her off, told her I had stuff I needed to do.

Then Jere got up and went to the podium. "Thanks, Mona," he said. "Today means so much to my family, and I know it would have meant even more to my mom. The women's shelter was really important to her. Even when we weren't here in Cousins, she was still thinking about you guys. And she loved flowers. She used to say she needed them to breathe. She would be so honored by this garden."

It was a good speech. Our mom would have been proud to see him up there. I should have been up there with him. She would have really liked that. She would have liked the roses, too.

I watched Jere sit down in the first row in the seat next to Belly. I watched him take her hand. The muscles in my stomach clenched, and I moved behind a woman in a wide-brimmed hat.

This was a mistake. Coming back here was a mistake.

chapter *twenty-one*

The speeches were over, and everyone had gone outside and started milling around the garden.

"What kind of flowers do you want for the wedding?" Jeremiah asked me in a low voice.

I smiled and shrugged. "Pretty ones?" What did I know about flowers? What did I know about weddings, for that matter? I hadn't been to many, only my cousin Beth's that time I was a flower girl and our neighbor's. But I liked this game we were playing. It was like pretend, but real.

Then I saw him. Standing there in the back was Conrad, in a gray suit. I stared, and he lifted his hand in a wave. I lifted mine, but I didn't move. Couldn't move.

Next to me, I heard Jeremiah clear his throat. I started. I'd forgotten he was standing next to me. For those couple of seconds, I forgot everything.

Then Mr. Fisher was pushing past us, striding over to him. They embraced. My mother swept Conrad into her arms, then my brother came up from behind and pounded him on the back. Jeremiah made his way over too.

I was last. I found myself walking over to them. "Hi," I said. I didn't know what to do with my hands. I left them at my sides.

He said, "Hi." Then he opened his arms up wide and gave me a look that was a lot like a dare. Hesitantly, I stepped into them. He crushed me in a bear hug and lifted me off the ground a little. I squealed and held down my skirt. Everyone laughed. When Conrad set me back down, I moved closer to Jere. He wasn't laughing.

"Conrad's glad to have his little sister around again," Mr. Fisher said in a jovial kind of way. I wondered if he even knew that Conrad and I had once dated. Probably not. It had only been six months. It was nothing compared to the time Jeremiah and I had spent together.

"How have you been, little sis?" Conrad asked. He had that look on his face. Part mocking, part mischievous. I knew that look; I'd seen it so many times.

"Great," I said, looking at Jeremiah. "We're really great."

Jeremiah didn't look back at me. Instead he pulled his phone out of his pocket and said, "I'm starving." I could feel a little knot in my stomach. Was he mad at me?

"Let's get some pictures by the garden before we go," my mother said.

Mr. Fisher clapped his hands and rubbed them together. Putting his arms around Jeremiah and Conrad, he said, "I want a picture with the Fishermen!" which made us all laugh—this time Jeremiah, too. That was one of Mr. Fisher's oldest and corniest jokes. Whenever he and the boys would come back from fishing trips, he would yell, "The Fishermen have returned!"

By Susannah's rose garden, we took pictures of Jeremiah and Mr. Fisher and Conrad, then one with Steven, too, then one with me and my mother and Steven and Jeremiah—all sorts of combinations. Jere said, "I want one of just me and Belly," and I was relieved. We stood in front of the roses, and right before my mother snapped the picture, Jeremiah kissed me on the cheek.

"That's a nice one," my mother said. Then she said, "Let's have one of all the kids."

We stood together—Jeremiah, Conrad, me, Steven. Conrad slung his arm around Jeremiah's and my shoulders. It was all like no time had passed. The summer kids together again.

I rode with Jeremiah to the restaurant. My mother and Steven took one car, Mr. Fisher and Conrad both drove separately.

"Maybe we shouldn't tell them today," I said suddenly. "Maybe we should wait."

Jeremiah turned down the music. "What do you mean?"

"I don't know. Maybe today should just be about Susannah, and family. Maybe we should wait."

"I don't want to have to wait. You and me getting married *is* about family. It's about our two families coming together. As one." Grinning, he grabbed my hand and lifted it in the air. "I want you to be able to wear your ring, right now, loud and proud."

"I *am* loud and proud," I said.

"Then let's just do it like we planned."

"Okay."

As we pulled into the restaurant parking lot, Jeremiah said to me, "Don't have hurt feelings if—you know, if he says anything."

I blinked. "Who?"

"My dad. You know how he is. You can't take it personally, okay?"

I nodded.

We walked into the restaurant holding hands. Everyone else was already there and seated at a round table.

I sat down, Jeremiah on my left and my brother on my right. I grabbed the bread basket and took a roll. I smeared it with butter before I stuffed most of it into my mouth.

Steven shook his head at me. *Pig*, he mouthed.

Glaring at him, I said, "I didn't eat breakfast."

"I ordered a bunch of appetizers," Mr. Fisher told me.

"Thanks, Mr. Fisher," I said, my mouth partly full.

He smiled. "Belly, we're all adults here. I think you should call me Adam now. No more Mr. Fisher."

Underneath the table, Jeremiah gave my thigh a squeeze. I almost laughed out loud. Then I had another thought—like, was I going to have to call Mr. Fisher "Dad" after we were married? I would have to talk to Jeremiah about that one.

"I'll try," I said. Mr. Fisher looked at me expectantly, and I added, "Adam."

Steven asked Conrad, "So why don't you ever leave California?"

"I'm here, aren't I?"

"Yeah, for, like, the first time since you left, practically." Steven nudged him and lowered his voice. "You got a girl out there?"

"No," Conrad said. "No girl."

The champagne arrived then, and when all our glasses were full, Mr. Fisher tapped his knife to his glass. "I'd like to make a toast," he said.

My mother rolled her eyes just barely. Mr. Fisher was famous for making speeches, but today actually called for one.

"I want to thank everyone for coming together today to celebrate Susannah. It's a special day, and I'm glad we can share it together." Mr. Fisher lifted his glass. "To Suz."

Nodding, my mother said, "To Beck."

We all clinked glasses and drank, and before I could put mine down, Jeremiah gave me this look like, Get ready, it's happening.

My stomach lurched. I took another gulp of my champagne and nodded.

"I have something to say," Jeremiah announced.

While everyone was waiting to hear what it was, I snuck a look over at Conrad. He had his arm draped over the back of Steven's chair, and they'd been laughing about something. His face was easy and relaxed.

I had this wild impulse to stop Jeremiah, to clap my hand over his mouth and keep him from saying it. Everybody was so happy. This was going to wreck it.

"I'll just go ahead and warn you—it's really good news." Jeremiah flashed a smile at everyone, and I braced myself. He was being too glib, I thought. My mother wouldn't like that. "I asked Belly to marry me, and she said yes. She said yes! We're getting married this August!"

It was like the restaurant got really quiet all of a sudden, like all the noise and chatter got sucked out of the room. Everything just stopped. I looked across the table, at my mother. Her face was ashen. Steven choked on the water he was drinking. Coughing, he said, "What the?" And Conrad, his face was completely blank.

It was surreal.

The waiter came by then with the appetizers—calamari and cocktail shrimp and a tower of oysters. "Are you guys ready to order your entrees?" he asked, rearranging the table so there was room for everything.

His voice tight, Mr. Fisher said, "I think we need a few more minutes," and glanced at my mother.

She looked dazed. She opened, then closed her mouth. Then she looked right at me and asked, "Are you pregnant?"

I felt all the blood rush to my cheeks. Beside me, I could feel rather than hear Jeremiah choke.

My mother's voice shook as she said shrilly, "I don't believe this. How many times have we discussed contraception, Isabel?"

I could not have been more mortified. I looked at Mr. Fisher, who was beet red, and then I looked at the waiter, who was pouring water for the table next to ours. Our eyes met. I was pretty sure he'd been in my psychology class. "Mom, I'm not pregnant!"

Earnestly, Jeremiah said, "Laurel, I swear to you it's nothing like that."

My mother ignored him. She looked only at me. "Then what is happening here? Where is this coming from?"

My lips felt really dry all of a sudden. Fleetingly, I thought of what had led up to Jeremiah's proposal, and just as quickly the thought flitted away. None of that mattered anymore. What mattered was that we were in love. I said, "We want to get married, Mom."

"You're too young," she said in a flat voice. "You're both far too young."

Jeremiah coughed. "Laur, we love each other, and we want to be together."

"You *are* together," my mother snapped. Then she turned to Mr. Fisher, her eyes narrowed. "Did you know about this?"

"Calm down, Laurel. They're joking. You were joking, right?"

Jere and I shared a look before he said in a soft voice, "No, we're not joking."

My mother swallowed the rest of her champagne, emptying her glass. "You two are not getting married, period. You're both still in school, for God's sake. It's ridiculous."

Clearing his throat, Mr. Fisher said, "Maybe after you kids both graduate, we can discuss it again."

"A few years after you graduate," my mother put in.

"Right," Mr. Fisher said.

"Dad . . . ," Jeremiah began.

The server was back at Mr. Fisher's shoulder before Jeremiah could finish whatever it was he was going to say. He just stood there for a moment looking awkward before asking, "Do you have any questions about the menu? Or, ah, are we just doing appetizers today?"

"We'll just take the check," my mother said, tight lipped.

There was all this food on the table and no one

was touching it, no one was saying anything. I was right before. This was a mistake, a tactical error of epic proportions. We never should have told them like this. Now they were a team, united against us. We barely got a word in edgewise.

I reached into my purse, and under the tablecloth, I put my engagement ring on. It was the only thing I could think to do. When I reached for my water glass, Jeremiah saw the ring and squeezed my knee again. My mother saw too—her eyes flashed, and she looked away.

Mr. Fisher paid the bill, and for once my mother didn't argue. We all stood up. Quickly, Steven filled a cloth napkin with shrimp. And then we were leaving, me trailing my mother, Jeremiah following Mr. Fisher. Behind me, I heard Steven whispering to Conrad. "Holy shit, man. This is crazy. Did *you* know about this?"

I heard Conrad tell him no. Outside, he hugged my mother good-bye and then got in his car and drove away. He didn't look back once.

When we got to our car, I asked my mother very quietly, "Can I have the keys?"

"What for?"

I wet my lips. "I need to get my book bag out of the trunk. I'm going with Jeremiah, remember?"

I could see my mother struggle to hold her temper. She said, "No, you're not. You're coming home with us."

"But Mom—"

Before I could finish, she'd already handed the keys to Steven and climbed into the passenger seat. She closed the door.

I looked at Jeremiah helplessly. Mr. Fisher was already in his car, and Jeremiah was hanging back, waiting. More than anything, I wished I could leave with him. I was really, really scared to get into the car with my mother.

I was in trouble like I had never known.

"Get in the car, Belly," Steven said. "Don't make it worse."

"You'd better go," Jeremiah said.

I ran over to him and hugged him tight. "I'll call you tonight," he whispered into my hair.

"If I'm still alive," I whispered back.

Then I walked away from him and climbed into the backseat.

Steven started the car, his napkin a white bundle in his lap. My mother caught my eye in the rearview mirror and said, "You're returning that ring, Isabel."

If I backed down now, everything was lost. I had to be strong.

"I'm not returning it," I said.

chapter *twenty-two*

My mother and I didn't speak to each other for a week. I avoided her, and she ignored me. I worked at Behrs, mostly to get out of the house. I ate lunch and dinner there. After my shifts, I went over to Taylor's, and when I got home, I talked to Jeremiah on the phone. He begged me to at least try to talk to my mother. I knew he was worried that she hated him now, and I assured him that he wasn't the one she was mad at. That was all me.

One night after a late shift at the restaurant, I was on my way to my room when I stopped short. I heard the muffled sound of my mother crying behind her closed door. I was frozen to the spot, my heart thudding in my chest. Standing outside her door, listening to her weep, I was ready to give it all up. In that moment I would have done anything, said anything, to make her stop crying.

In that moment she had me. My hand was on the door-knob, and the words were right there, on the tip of my tongue—Okay, I won't do it.

But then it got quiet. She'd stopped crying on her own. I waited a little longer, and when I didn't hear anything more, I let go of the doorknob and went to my room. In the dark I took off my work clothes and got into bed, and I cried too.

I woke up to the smell of my father's Turkish coffee. For just those few seconds right in between sleep and wake-fulness, I was ten again, and my dad still lived with us and the biggest thing I had to worry about was my math homework. I started to fall back to sleep, and then I woke up with a start.

There could only be one reason my dad was here. My mother had told him. I'd wanted to be the one to tell him, to explain. She'd beaten me to it. I was mad, but at the same time I felt glad. Her telling my father meant that she was finally taking this seriously.

After I showered, I headed downstairs. They were sitting in the living room drinking coffee. My dad had on his weekend clothes—jeans and a plaid short-sleeved shirt. And a belt, always a belt.

"Morning," I said.

"Have a seat," my mother said, setting her mug down on a coaster.

I sat. My hair was still wet, and I was trying to work my comb through the tangles.

Clearing his throat, my father said, "So, your mother told me what's going on."

"Dad, I wanted to tell you myself, I really did. Mom beat me to the punch." I threw her a pointed look, but she didn't appear the least bit bothered by it.

"I'm not in favor of this either, Belly. I think you're too young." He cleared his throat again. "We've discussed it, and if you want to live with Jeremiah in an apartment this fall, we'll allow it. You'll have to chip in if it costs more than the dorms, but we'll pay what we've been paying."

I wasn't expecting that. A compromise. I was sure it had been my dad's idea, but I couldn't take the deal.

"Dad, I don't just want to live in an apartment with Jeremiah. That's not why we're getting married."

"Then why *are* you getting married?" my mother asked me.

"We love each other. We've thought it through, we really have."

My mother gestured at my left hand. "Who paid for that ring? I know Jeremiah doesn't have a job."

I put my hand in my lap. "He used his credit card," I said.

"His credit card that Adam pays for. If Jeremiah can't afford a ring, he has no business buying one."

"It didn't cost much." I had no idea how much the ring had cost, but the diamond was so little, I figured it couldn't have been *that* expensive.

Sighing, my mother glanced over at my father and then back at me. "You might not believe me when I say this, but when your father and I got married, we were very much in love. Very, very much in love. We went into marriage with the best of intentions. But all of that just wasn't enough to sustain us."

Their love for each other, Steven and me, our family— none of it was enough to make their marriage work. I knew all of that already.

"Do you regret it?" I asked her.

"Belly, it isn't as simple as that."

I interrupted her. "Do you regret our family? Do you regret me and Steven?"

Sighing deeply, she said, "No."

"Dad, do you?"

"Belly, no. Of course not. That's not what your mother's trying to say."

"Jeremiah and I aren't you and Mom. We've known each other our whole lives." I tried to appeal to my father. "Dad, your cousin Martha got married young, and she and Bert have been married for, like, thirty years! It can work, I know it can. Jeremiah and I will make it work just like they did. We're going to be happy. We just want you guys to be happy for us. Please be happy for us."

My father rubbed his beard in a way I knew well—he was going to defer to my mother the way he always did. Any second, he would look at her with a question in his eyes. It was all up to her now. Actually, it had always been up to her.

We both looked at her. My mother was the judge. That was the way it worked in our family. She closed her eyes briefly and then said, "I can't support you in this decision, Isabel. If you go forward with this wedding, I won't support it. I won't be there."

It knocked the wind out of me. Even though I was expecting it, her continued disapproval . . . still. Still, I thought she'd come around, at least a little.

"Mom," I said, my voice breaking, "come on."

Looking pained, my father said, "Belly, let's all just think on this some more, okay? This is very sudden for us."

I ignored him and looked only at my mother. Pleadingly, I said, "Mom? I know you don't mean that."

She shook her head. "I do mean it."

"Mom, you can't not be at my wedding. That's crazy." I tried to sound calm, like I wasn't on the verge of out-and-out hysteria.

"No, what's crazy is the idea of a teenager getting married." She pressed her lips together. "I don't know what to say to get through to you. How do I get through to you, Isabel?"

"You can't," I said.

My mother leaned forward, her eyes fixed on me. "Don't do this."

"It's already decided. I'm marrying Jeremiah." I stood up jerkily. "If you can't be happy for me, then maybe—maybe it's best you don't come."

I was already at the staircase when my dad called out, "Belly, wait."

I stopped, and then I heard my mother say, "Let her go."

When I was in my room, I called Jeremiah. The first thing he said was, "Do you want me to talk to her?"

"That won't help. I'm telling you, she's made up her mind. I know her. She won't budge. At least not right now."

He was silent. "Then what do you want to do?"

"I don't know." I started to cry.

"Do you want to postpone the wedding?"

"No!"

"Then what should we do?"

Wiping my face, I said, "I guess just move ahead with the wedding. Start planning."

As soon as we got off the phone, I started seeing things more clearly. I just needed to separate emotion from reason. Refusing to go to the wedding was my mother's trump card. It was the only leg she had to stand on. And she was bluffing. She had to be bluffing. No matter how upset or disappointed she was in me, I couldn't believe that she would miss her only daughter's wedding. I just couldn't.

All there was to do now was to steamroll ahead and set this wedding in motion. With or without my mother by my side, this was happening.

chapter *twenty-three*

I was folding my laundry when Steven knocked on my door later that night. As usual he only gave me a couple of seconds before opening it; he never waited for me to say "come in." He came into the room and shut the door behind him. Steven stood in my room awkwardly, leaning against the wall, his arms folded against his chest.

"What?" I said. Although I already knew.

"Sooo . . . are you and Jere serious about this?"

I stacked some T-shirts into a pile. "Yes."

Steven crossed the room and sat at my desk, absorbing my answer for a minute. Then he faced me, straddling the chair, and said, "You realize that's insane, right? We're not living in the foothills of West Virginia. There's no reason you have to get married so young."

"What do you know about West Virginia?" I scoffed. "You've never even been there."

"That's besides the point."

"What is your point?"

"My point is, you guys are too young."

"Did Mom send you up here to talk to me?"

"No," he said, and I knew he was lying. "I'm just worried about you."

I stared him down.

"Okay, yeah, she did," he admitted. "But I would have come up anyway."

"You're not going to change my mind."

"Listen, nobody knows you two better than me." He stopped, weighing his words. "I love Jere—he's like a brother to me. But you're my little sister. You come first. This whole marriage idea—I'm sorry, but I think it's stupid. If you guys love each other that much, you can wait a couple of years to be together. And if you can't, you for sure shouldn't be getting married."

I felt both touched and annoyed. Steven never said things like "You come first." But then he called me stupid, which was more like him.

"I don't expect you to understand," I said. I folded then refolded another T-shirt. "Jeremiah wants you and Conrad to be his best men."

Steven's face broke into a smile. "He does?"

"Yeah," I said.

Steven looked really happy, but then he caught me looking at him, and he wiped his smile away. "I don't think Mom will let me be in the wedding."

"Steven, you're twenty-one years old. You can decide that for yourself."

He frowned. I could tell I'd injured his pride. He said, "Well, I still don't think it's your smartest move."

"Noted," I said. "I'm still doing it."

"Oh, man, Mom's gonna kill me. I was supposed to talk you out of getting married, not get roped into the wedding party," Steven said, getting up.

I hid my smile. That is, until Steven added, "Con and I had better start planning the bachelor party."

Quickly, I said, "Jere doesn't want any of that."

Steven puffed up his chest. "You don't get a say in it, Belly. You're a girl. This is man stuff."

"*Man* stuff?"

Grinning, he shut my door.

chapter *twenty-four*

Despite what I'd said to Steven, I still found myself waiting for my mother. Waiting for her to come around, waiting for her to give in. I didn't want to start planning the wedding until she said yes. But when days passed and she refused to discuss it, I knew I couldn't wait any longer.

Thank God for Taylor.

She brought over a big white binder with clippings from wedding magazines and checklists and all kinds of stuff. "I was saving this for my wedding, but we can use it for yours, too," she said.

All I had was one of my mother's yellow legal pads. I had written WEDDING at the top and made a list of things I needed to do. The list looked pretty skimpy, next to Taylor's binder.

We were sitting on my bed, papers and bride maga-zines all around us. Taylor was all business.

She said, "First things first. We have to find you a dress. August is really, really soon."

"It doesn't feel *that* soon," I said.

"Well, it is. Two months to plan a wedding is nothing. In weddingspeak that's, like, tomorrow."

"Well, I guess since the wedding is going to be simple, the dress should be too," I said.

Taylor frowned. "How simple?"

"Really simple. As simple as it gets. Nothing poofy or frou frou."

She nodded to herself. "I can picture it. It's very Cindy Crawford wedding-on-the-beach, very Carolyn Bessette."

"Yeah, sounds good," I said. I had no idea what either of their wedding dresses looked like. I didn't even know who Carolyn Bessette was. After I had the dress, it would feel more real, I would be able to visualize it happening. Right now it still felt too abstract.

"What about shoes?"

I gave her a look. "Like I'm gonna wear heels on the beach. I can barely walk in heels on level ground."

Taylor ignored me. "What about my bridesmaid dress?"

I pushed some magazines onto the carpet so I could lie down. I stretched my legs as high as I could and put my feet up on the wall. "I was thinking mustard yellow. Maybe in a satiny kind of material." Taylor hated mustard yellow.

"Mustard yellow satin," Taylor repeated, nodding and trying hard to keep the disgust off her face. I could tell she was torn between her vanity and her credo, which was, the Bride is always right. "That could maybe work with Anika's skin tone. I'm more of a spring, but if I started tanning now, it could work."

I laughed. "I'm kidding. You can wear whatever you want."

"Dork!" she said, looking relieved. She slapped my thigh. "You're so immature! I can't believe you're getting married!"

"Me neither."

"But I guess it makes sense, in a Twilight Zone kind of way. You and Jere have known each other for, like, a grillion years. It's meant to be."

"How long is a grillion years?"

"It's forever." In the air she spelled out my initials. "B.C. + J.F. forever."

"Forever," I echoed happily. Forever I could do. Me and Jere.

chapter *twenty-five*

On my way out to meet Taylor at the mall the next day, I stopped by my mother's office. "I'm going to look for a dress," I said, standing in her doorway.

She stopped typing and looked over at me. "Good luck," she said.

"Thanks." I supposed there were worse things she could have said than "good luck," but the thought didn't make me feel any better.

The formal-wear store at the mall was packed with girls looking for prom dresses with their mothers. I didn't expect to feel the pang in my chest when I saw them. Girls were supposed to go wedding dress shopping with their mothers. They were supposed to step out of the dressing room in just the right dress, and the mother would tear up and say, "That's the one." I was pretty sure that was the way it was supposed to be.

"Isn't it a little late in the year for prom?" I asked Taylor. "Wasn't ours in, like, May?"

"My sister told me they had to push back prom this year because of some scandal with the assistant principal," she explained. "All the prom money went missing or something. So now it's a grom. Graduation-prom."

I laughed. "Grom."

"Also, the private schools always have their prom later, remember? Collegiate, St. Joe's."

"I only went to one prom," I reminded her. One had been more than enough for me.

I wandered around the store and found one dress I liked—it was strapless, blinding white. I'd never known there were degrees of white before; I'd just thought white was white. When I found Taylor, she had a whole stack of dresses on her arm. We had to wait in line for a dressing room.

The girl in front of me told her mother, "I will freak out if someone wears the same dress as me."

Taylor and I rolled our eyes at each other. *I will freak out,* Taylor mouthed.

It seemed like we waited in that line forever.

"Try this one on first," Taylor ordered when it was my turn.

Dutifully, I obeyed her.

"Come out," Taylor yelled from her chair by the three-way mirror. She was camped out with the other mothers.

"I don't think I like it," I called out. "It's too sparkly. I look like Glinda the good witch or something."

"Just come out and let me see you!"

I came out, and there were already a couple of other girls at the mirror, checking themselves out from the back. I stood behind them.

Then the girl from earlier stepped out in the same dress I had on but in a champagne color. She saw me, and right away she asked, "Which prom are you going to?"

Taylor and I looked at each other in the mirror. Taylor was covering her mouth, giggling. I said, "I'm not going to prom."

Taylor said, "She's getting married!"

The girl's mouth hung open. "How old are you? You look so young."

"I'm not that young," I said. "I'm nineteen." I wouldn't be nineteen until August, but nineteen sounded a lot older than eighteen.

"Oh," she said. "I thought we were, like, the same age."

I looked at us in the mirror as we stood there in the same dress. I thought we looked the same age too. I saw her mother looking at me and whispering to the lady next to her, and I could feel myself blush.

Taylor saw too and said, loudly, "You can hardly even tell she's three months pregnant."

The woman gasped. She shook her head at me, and I gave her a little shrug. Then Taylor grabbed my hand, and we ran back to my dressing room, laughing.

"You're a good friend," I said as she unzipped me.

We looked at each other in the mirror, me in my white dress and her in her cutoffs and flip-flops. I felt like I was going to cry. But then Taylor saved it—she made me laugh instead. She crossed her eyes and stuck her tongue out sideways. It felt good to laugh again.

Three more stores later, we sat in the food court, still no dress. Taylor ate french fries, and I ate frozen yogurt with rainbow sprinkles. My feet hurt, and I was already wanting to go home. The day wasn't turning out to be as fun as I'd hoped it would be.

Taylor leaned across the table and dipped an already-ketchupped french fry into my frozen yogurt. I snatched the cup away from her.

"Taylor! That's disgusting."

She shrugged. "This coming from the girl who puts powdered sugar on Cap'n Crunch?" Handing me a fry, she said, "Just try it."

I dipped it into the cup, careful not to get any sprinkles on it, because that would just be too gross. I popped the fry into my mouth. Not bad. Swallowing, I said, "What if we can't find a dress?"

"We'll find a dress," she assured me, handing me another fry. "Don't get all Debbie Downer on me yet."

She was right. We found it at the next store. It was the last one I tried on. Everything else had been only so-so or too expensive. This dress was long and white and silky and something you could wear on the beach. It was not that expensive, which was important. But most important of all, when I looked in the mirror, I could picture myself getting married in it.

Nervously, I stepped out, smoothing the dress down on my sides. I looked up at her. "What do you think?"

Her eyes were shining. "It's perfect. Just perfect."

"You think?"

"Come look at yourself in this mirror and you tell me, beotch."

Giggling, I stepped up on the platform and stared at myself in the three-way mirror. This was it. This was the one.

chapter *twenty-six*

That night I tried on my dress again and called Jeremiah. "I found my dress," I told him. "I'm wearing it right now."

"What's it look like?"

"It's a surprise. But I promise, it's really pretty. Taylor and I found it at the fifth store we went to. It didn't even cost that much." I ran my hand along the silky fabric. "It fits me perfectly, so I won't have to get alterations or anything."

"So why do you sound so sad, then?"

I sat down on the floor, hugging my knees to my chest. "I don't know. Maybe 'cause my mom wasn't there to help me pick it out. . . . I thought buying a wedding dress was supposed to be this special thing you do with your mom, and she wasn't there. It was nice with Taylor, but I wish my mom had been there too."

Jeremiah was quiet. Then he said, "Did you ask her to go with you?"

"No, not really. But she knew I wanted her there. I just hate that she's not a part of this." I'd left my bedroom door open, hoping my mom might walk by, might see me in the dress and stop. She hadn't so far.

"She'll come around."

"I hope so. I don't know if I can picture getting married without my mom there, you know?"

I heard Jere let out a little sigh. "Yeah, me either," he said, and I knew he was thinking of Susannah.

The next morning, my mother and I were eating breakfast, my mother with her yogurt with muesli and me with my frozen waffles, when the doorbell rang.

My mother looked up from her newspaper. "Are you expecting someone?" she asked me.

I shook my head and got up to see who it was. I opened the front door, figuring it would be Taylor with more bridal magazines. Instead, it was Jeremiah. He had a bouquet of lilies, and he had on a nice shirt, white button-down with faint blue checks.

I clapped my hands over my mouth in delight. "What are you doing here?" I shrieked from behind my hands.

He hugged me to him. I could smell McDonald's coffee on his breath. He must have woken up really early to get here. Jeremiah loved McDonald's breakfasts but he could never wake up early enough to get one. He said, "Don't get too excited. These aren't for you. Is Laurel here?"

I felt swoony and dazed. "She's eating breakfast," I said. "Come on in."

I opened the door for him, and he followed me inside to the kitchen. Brightly, I said, "Mom, look who's here!"

My mother looked astonished, her spoon halfway to her mouth. "Jeremiah!"

Jeremiah walked over to her, flowers in hand. "I just had to come and greet my future mother-in-law properly," he said, grinning his impish grin. He kissed her on the cheek and set the flowers by her bowl of yogurt.

I was watching closely. If anybody could charm my mother, it was Jeremiah. Already I could feel the tension in our house being lifted.

She smiled a smile that looked brittle, but it was a smile nonetheless. She stood up. "I'm glad you came," she said. "I've been wanting to talk to the both of you."

Jeremiah rubbed his hands together. "All righty. Let's do this. Belly, get over here. Group hug first."

My mother tried not to laugh as Jeremiah gave her a bear hug. He motioned for me to join in, and I came up behind my mother and hugged her around the waist. She couldn't help it: a laugh escaped. "All right, all right. Let's go into the living room. Jere, have you eaten?"

I answered for him. "Egg McMuffin, right, Jere?"

He winked at me. "You know me so well."

My mother had already stepped into the living room, her back to us.

"I can smell McDonald's on your breath," I told him in a low voice.

He clapped his hand over his mouth, looking self-conscious, which was rare for him. "Does it smell bad?" he asked me.

I felt so much tenderness toward him in that moment. "No," I told him. "Not at all."

The three of us sat in the living room, Jeremiah and I on the couch, my mother in an armchair facing us. Everything was going so well. He had made my mother laugh. I hadn't seen her laugh or smile since we'd told her. I started to feel hopeful, like this might actually work.

The first thing she said was, "Jeremiah, you know I love you. I want nothing but the best for you. That's why I can't support what you two are doing."

Jeremiah leaned forward. "Laur—"

My mother held up her hand. "You're just too young. Both of you. You're both still gestating and becoming the people you will one day be. You're still children. You aren't ready for a commitment like this. I'm talking about a lifetime here, Jeremiah."

Eagerly, he said, "Laurel, I want to be with Belly for a lifetime. I can commit to that, easy."

My mother shook her head. "And that's how I know you're not ready, Jeremiah. You take things too lightly. This isn't the kind of thing you undertake on a whim. This is serious." The condescension in her voice really pissed me off. I was eighteen years old, not eight, and Jeremiah was nineteen. We were old enough to know that marriage was serious. We'd seen the way our parents had screwed up their own marriages. We weren't going to make the same mistakes. But I didn't say anything. I knew that if I got mad or tried to argue, it would only prove her point. So I just sat there. "I want you two to wait. I want Belly to finish school. When she graduates, if you two still feel the same way, do it then. But only after she graduates. If Beck was here, she'd agree with me."

"I think she'd be really happy for us," Jeremiah said.

Before my mother could contradict him, he added, "Belly will still finish college on time, I can promise you that. I'll take good care of her. Just give us your blessing." He reached out and touched her hand and gave it a playful shake. "Come on, Laur. You know you've always wanted me for a son-in-law."

My mother looked pained. "Not like this, hon. I'm sorry."

There was a long, awkward pause. As the three of sat there, I could feel myself start to tear up. Jeremiah put his arm around me and clasped my shoulder, then he let go.

"Does this mean you aren't coming to the wedding?" I asked her.

Shaking her head, she said, "Isabel, what wedding? You don't have the money to pay for a wedding."

"That's for us to worry about, not you," I said. "I just want to know, are you coming?"

"I already gave you my answer. No, I won't be there."

"How can you say that?" I let out a breath, trying to keep calm. "You're just mad that you don't get a say in this. You don't get a say in what happens, and it's killing you."

"Yes, it is killing me!" she snapped. "Watching you make such a stupid decision is killing me."

My mother fixed her eyes on me, and I turned my head away from her, my knees shaking. I couldn't listen to her anymore. She was poisoning our good news with all her doubts and negativity. She was twisting everything.

I stood up. "Then I'll leave. You won't have to watch anymore."

Jeremiah looked startled. "Come on, Bells, sit down."

"I can't stay here," I said.

My mother didn't say a word. She just sat there, her back ramrod straight.

I walked out of the living room and up the stairs.

In my room I packed quickly, throwing a stack of T-shirts and underwear into a suitcase. I was throwing my toiletries bag on top of the heap when Jeremiah came into my room. He closed the door behind him.

He sat down on my bed. "What just happened?" he asked, still looking dazed.

I didn't answer him, I kept packing.

"What are you doing?" he asked me.

"What does it look like?"

"Okay, but do you have a plan?"

I zipped up my suitcase. "Yes, I have a plan. I'm staying at the Cousins house until the wedding. I can't deal with her."

Jeremiah sucked in his breath. "Are you serious?"

"You heard her. She isn't changing her mind. This is the way she wants it."

He hesitated. "I don't know. . . . What about your job?"

"You're the one who told me I should quit. It's better this way. I can plan the wedding better in Cousins than I can here." I was sweating as I heaved up my suitcase. "If she can't get on board this train, then that's too bad. Because this is happening."

Jeremiah tried to take the suitcase from me, but I told him not to bother. I lugged it down the stairs and to the car without a word to or from my mother. She didn't ask where we were going, and she didn't ask when I was coming back.

On the way out of town, we stopped at Behrs. Jere waited for me in his car while I went inside. If I hadn't just had a fight with my mother, I never would have had the nerve to quit like that. Even though people came and went all the time at Behrs, especially students . . . still. I went straight back to the kitchen and found my manager, Stacey, and told her I was sorry, but as it turned out I was getting married in two months and I couldn't keep working there. Stacey eyed my stomach and then my ring finger and said, "Congratulations, Isabel. Just so you know, there's always a place for you here at Behrs."

Alone in my car again, I cried loud, ragged sobs. I cried until my throat hurt. I was mad at my mom, but bigger than that was this overwhelming, heavy sadness. I was grown up enough to do things on my own, without her. I could get married, I could quit my job. I was a big girl now. I didn't have to ask for her permission. My mother was no longer all powerful. Part of me wished she still could be.

chapter twenty-seven

We were half an hour from Cousins when Jeremiah called and said, "Conrad's been staying in Cousins."

My whole body went stiff. We were at a stoplight, and Jeremiah's car was in front of mine. "Since when?"

"Since last week. He just stayed after the whole thing at the restaurant. He came back once to get his stuff, but I think he's gonna spend the summer out here."

"Oh," I said. "Do you think he'll mind that I'm staying there?"

I could hear Jere hesitate. "No, I don't think he'll mind. I just wish I could be there too. If it wasn't for that stupid internship, I could be. Maybe I should just quit."

"You can't. Your dad will kill you."

"Yeah, I know." I heard him hesitate again, and then he said, "I don't feel right about the way we left things with your mom. Maybe you should go back home, Bells."

"It won't work. We'll just fight again." The light turned green. "You know, I actually think this could be for the best. It'll give us both space."

"If you say so," Jeremiah said, but I could tell he didn't completely agree.

"Let's talk more when we get to the house," I said, and we hung up.

This news that Conrad was in Cousins left me feeling uneasy. Maybe staying at the summer house wasn't the answer.

But then, when I pulled into the empty driveway, I felt such incredible relief to be back. Home, I was back home.

The house looked the same, tall and gray and white. It made me feel the same. Like I was right where I belonged. Like I could breathe again.

I was sitting in Jeremiah's lap on a lounge chair when we heard a car pull up. It was Conrad, getting out of the car with a bag of groceries. He looked taken aback to see us sitting there on the deck. I stood up and waved.

Jeremiah stretched his hands behind his head and leaned back onto his chair. "Hey, Con."

"What's up," he said, walking over to us. "What are you guys doing here?"

Conrad set down the grocery bag and took a seat next to Jeremiah's, and I just sort of hovered above them.

"Wedding stuff," Jeremiah said vaguely.

"Wedding stuff," Conrad repeated. "So you guys are really doing it?"

"Hell yeah we are." Jeremiah pulled me back onto his lap. "Right, wifey?"

"Don't call me wifey," I said, wrinkling my nose. "Gross."

Conrad ignored me. "Does that mean Laurel's changed her mind?" he asked Jere.

"Not yet, but she will," Jeremiah said, and I didn't correct him.

I sat perched there for about twenty more seconds before I twisted out of his arms and stood up again. "I'm starving," I said, leaning down and poking around Conrad's grocery bag. "Did you buy anything good?"

Conrad gave me his bemused half smile. "No Cheetos or frozen pizza for you in here. Sorry. I got stuff for dinner, though. I'll cook something for us."

He got up, took the grocery bag, and went into the house.

For dinner, Conrad made a tomato, basil, and avocado salad, and he grilled chicken breasts. We ate outside on the deck.

With a mouth full of chicken, Jeremiah said, "Wow, I'm impressed. Since when do you cook?"

"Since I've been living on my own. This is pretty much all I eat. Chicken. Every day." Conrad pushed the salad bowl toward me, not looking up. "Did you get enough?"

"Yeah. Thanks, Conrad. This is all really good."

"Really good," Jeremiah echoed.

Conrad only shrugged, but the tips of his ears turned pink, and I knew he was pleased.

I poked Jeremiah in the arm with my fork. "You could learn a thing or two."

He poked me back. "So could you." He took a big bite of salad before announcing, "Belly's gonna stay here until the wedding. Is that cool with you, Con?"

I could tell Conrad was surprised, because he didn't answer right away.

"I won't be in your way," I assured him. "I'll just be doing wedding stuff."

"It's fine. I don't care," he said.

I looked down at my plate. "Thanks," I said. So I'd been worried about nothing. Conrad didn't care if I was there or not. It wasn't like we would have to hang out with each other. He would do his own thing the way he always did, I would be busy planning the wedding, and Jeremiah would drive up every Friday to help. It would be fine.

After we finished eating dinner, Jeremiah suggested we all go get ice cream for dessert. Conrad declined, saying he would clean up. I said, "The cook shouldn't have to clean up," but he said he didn't mind.

Jere and I went into town, just the two of us. I got a scoop of cookies and cream and a scoop of cookie dough with sprinkles, in a waffle cone. Jeremiah got rainbow sherbet.

"Are you feeling better?" he asked me as we walked around the boardwalk. "About what happened with your mom?"

"Not really," I said. "I'd rather just not think about it anymore today."

Jeremiah nodded. "Whatever you want."

I changed the subject. "Did you figure out how many people you want to invite?" I asked.

"Yup." He started to tick names off on his fingers. "Josh, Redbird, Gabe, Alex, Sanchez, Peterson—"

"You can't invite everyone in your fraternity."

"They're my brothers," he said, looking wounded.

"I thought we said we were keeping it really small."

"So I'll just invite a few of them, then. Okay?"

"Okay. We still have to figure out food," I said, licking my way around the cone so it wouldn't drip.

"We could always get Con to grill some chicken," Jeremiah said with a laugh.

"He's going to be your best man. He can't be sweating over the grill."

"I was kidding."

"Did you ask him yet? To be your best man?"

"Not yet. I will, though." He leaned down and took a bite of my ice cream. He got some on his upper lip, like a milk mustache.

I bit the insides of my cheeks to keep from smiling.

"What's so funny?"

"Nothing."

When we got back to the house, Conrad was watching TV in the living room. When we sat down on the couch, he got up. "I'm gonna hit the sack," he said, stretching his arms over his head.

"It's, like, ten o'clock. Watch a movie with us," Jeremiah said.

"Nah, I'm gonna get up early tomorrow and surf. Wanna join me?"

Jeremiah glanced at me before saying, "Yeah, sounds good."

"I thought we were gonna work on the guest list in the morning," I said.

"I'll come back before you're even awake. Don't worry." To Conrad, he said, "Knock on my door when you're up."

Conrad hesitated. "I don't want to wake up Belly."

I could feel myself blush. "I don't mind," I said.

Since Jeremiah and I had become boyfriend and girlfriend, we'd only been at the summer house together once. That time, I slept in his room with him. We watched TV until he fell asleep, because he liked to sleep with the television on in the background. I couldn't fall asleep like that, so I waited until he did and then I turned it off. It felt kind of strange, sleeping in his bed when mine was just down the hall.

At college we slept in the same bed all the time, and that felt normal. But here at the summer house I just wanted to sleep in my own room, in my own bed. It was familiar to me. It made me feel like a little girl still on vacation with her whole family. My paper-thin sheets with the faded yellow rosebuds, my cherry wood dresser and vanity. I used to have two white twin beds, but Susannah got rid of them and put in what she'd called a "big girl bed." I loved that bed.

Conrad went upstairs, and I waited until I heard his bedroom door shut before I said, "Maybe I'll sleep in my room tonight."

"Why?" Jeremiah asked. "I promise I'll be quiet when I get up."

Carefully, I asked, "Aren't the bride and groom supposed to sleep in different beds before the wedding?"

"Yeah, but that's the night before the wedding. Not every night before the wedding." He looked hurt for a second, and then he said in his joking way, "Come on, you know I won't touch you."

Even though I knew he was only kidding, it still stung a little.

"It's not that. Sleeping in my own room makes me feel . . . normal. It's—it's different than at school. At school, sleeping with you next to me feels normal. But here I like remembering what it used to feel like." I searched his face to see if any of the hurt was still there. "Does that make sense at all?"

"I guess." Jeremiah looked unconvinced, and I started to wish I'd never brought it up.

I scooted closer to him, putting my feet in his lap. "You'll have me next to you every night for the rest of our lives."

"Yeah, I guess that'll be plenty," he said.

"Hey!" I said, kicking out my leg.

Jeremiah just smiled and put a pillow over my feet. Then he changed the channel and we watched TV without saying anything more about it. When it was time to go to bed, he went to his room, and I went to mine.

I slept better than I had in weeks.

chapter *twenty-eight*
CONRAD

I asked Jere if he wanted to surf because I wanted to get him alone so I could find out what the hell was going on. I hadn't talked to him since he made his grand announcement at the restaurant. But now that we were alone, I didn't know what to say.

We bobbed on our surfboards, waiting for the next wave. It had been slow out there so far.

I cleared my throat. "So how pissed is Laurel?"

"*Pissed*," Jere said, grimacing. "Belly and her had a pretty big fight yesterday."

"In front of you?"

"Yeah."

"Shit." I wasn't surprised, though. There was no way Laurel was going to be like, sure, I'll throw my teenaged daughter a wedding.

"Yeah, pretty much."

"What does Dad say about all this?"

He gave me a funny look. "Since when do you care what Dad says?"

I looked out toward the house. I hesitated before saying, "I don't know. If Laurel's against it and Dad's against it, maybe you shouldn't do it. I mean, you guys are still in college. You don't even have a job. When you think about it, it's kind of ridiculous." My voice trailed off. Jere was shooting daggers at me.

"Stay out of it, Conrad," he said. He was practically spitting.

"All right. Sorry. I didn't mean to . . . I'm sorry."

"I never asked for your opinion. This is between me and Belly."

I said, "You're right. Forget it."

Jeremiah didn't answer. He looked over his shoulder, and then he started to paddle away. As the wave crested, he popped up and rode it to shore.

I punched my hand through the water. I wanted to kick his ass. *This is between me and Belly*. Smug piece of shit.

He was marrying my girl, and I couldn't do anything about it. I just had to watch it happen, because he was my brother, because I promised. *Take care of him, Connie. I'm counting on you.*

chapter *twenty-nine*

When I got up the next morning, the boys were still surfing, so I took my binder and my legal pad and a glass of
milk out to the deck.

According to Taylor's checklist, we had to get the
guest list figured out before we could do anything else.
That made sense. Otherwise, how would we know how
much food we needed and everything?

So far, my list was short. Taylor, her mom, a couple
of the girls we'd grown up with—Marcy and Blair and
maybe Katie—Anika, my dad, Steven, and my mother.
And I didn't even know if my mother was coming. My
dad would—I knew he would. No matter what my
mother said, he'd be there. I wanted my grandma to
come too, but she'd moved out of her house in Florida
and into a nursing home the year before. She'd never

liked traveling, and now she couldn't. In her invitation I decided I would write a note promising to visit with Jeremiah over fall break.

That was pretty much it for me. I had a few cousins on my dad's side but none I was particularly close to.

Jeremiah had Conrad, three of his fraternity brothers like we agreed, his freshman-year roommate, and his dad. Last night Jere told me he could tell his dad was softening. He said Mr. Fisher asked about who was marrying us and how much we were planning on spending on this so-called wedding. Jere told him our budget. One thousand dollars. Mr. Fisher had snorted. To me, a thousand dollars was a lot of money. Last year, it took me the whole summer to save that much waitressing at Behrs.

Our guest list would be under twenty people. With twenty people we could have a clambake and feed everyone, easy. We could get a few kegs and some cheap champagne. Since we'd be marrying on the beach, we wouldn't even need decorations. Just some flowers for the picnic tables, or shells. Shells and flowers. I was on a roll with this wedding. Taylor was going to be proud of me.

I was writing down my ideas as Jeremiah came up the steps. The sun blazed behind him, so bright it hurt my eyes. "Morning," I said, squinting up at him. "Where's Con?"

"He's still out there." Jeremiah sat down next to me.

Grinning, he asked, "Aw, did you do all the work without me?" He was dripping wet. A drop of seawater splashed down on my notepad.

"You wish." I wiped at the water. "Hey, what do you think about a clambake?"

"I like a good clambake," he agreed.

"How many kegs do you think we'd need for twenty people?"

"If Peterson and Gomez are coming, that's two already."

I pointed my pen at his chest. "We said three brothers and that's it. Right?"

He nodded, and then he leaned forward and kissed me. His lips tasted salty, and his face was cool against my warm one.

I nuzzled his cheek before I broke away. "If you get Taylor's binder wet, she'll kill you," I warned, putting it behind me.

Jeremiah made a sad face, and then he took my arms and put them around his neck like we were slow dancing. "I can't wait to marry you," he murmured into my neck.

I giggled. I was super ticklish on my neck, and he knew it. He knew almost everything about me and he still loved me.

"And what about you?"

"What about me?"

He blew on my neck, and I burst out laughing. I tried

to wriggle away from him, but he wouldn't let me. Still giggling, I said, "Okay, I can't wait to marry you either."

Jere left later that afternoon. I walked him out to his car. Conrad's car wasn't in the driveway; I didn't know where he'd gone off to.

"Call me when you get home so I know you got there safe," I said.

He nodded. He was being quiet, which was unlike him. I guessed he was sad to be leaving so soon. I wished he could stay longer too. I really did.

I got on my tiptoes and gave him a big hug. "See you in five days," I said.

"See you in five days," he repeated.

I watched him drive off, my thumbs hooked in the belt loops of my cutoffs. When I couldn't see his car anymore, I headed back inside the house.

chapter *thirty*

That first week in Cousins, I steered clear of Conrad. I couldn't deal with one more person telling me that I was making a mistake, especially judgy Conrad. He didn't even have to say it with words; he could judge with his eyes. So I got up earlier than him and ate meals before he did. And when he watched TV in the living room, I stayed upstairs in my room addressing invitations and looking at wedding blogs that Taylor had bookmarked for me.

I doubt he even noticed. He was pretty busy too. He surfed, he hung out with friends, he worked on the house. I'd never have known he was handy if I didn't see it with my own two eyes—Conrad on a ladder checking the air-conditioning vents, Conrad repainting the mailbox. I saw it all from my bedroom window.

I was eating a strawberry Pop-Tart on the deck when

he came jogging up the steps. He'd been out all morning. His hair was sweaty, and he was wearing an old T-shirt from his high school football days and a pair of navy gym shorts.

"Hey," I said. "Where are you coming from?"

"The gym," Conrad said, walking past me. Then he stopped short. "Is that what you're eating for breakfast?"

I was munching around the edge of the Pop-Tart. "Yeah, but it's my last one. Sorry."

He ignored me. "I left cereal out on the counter. There's fruit in the fruit bowl too."

I shrugged. "I thought it was yours. I didn't want to eat your stuff without asking."

Impatiently, he said, "Then why didn't you ask?"

I was taken aback. "How could I ask when I've barely even seen you?"

We scowled at each other for about three seconds before I saw a smile tugging at the corners of his mouth. "Fair enough," he said, and his trace of a smile was already gone. He started to slide the glass door open, and then he turned and said, "Whatever I buy, you can eat."

"Same here," I said.

That almost-smile again. "You can keep your Pop-Tarts and your Funyuns and your Kraft mac and cheese all to yourself."

"Hey, I eat other stuff besides just junk," I protested.

"Sure you do," he said, and he went inside.

The next morning, the cereal box was out on the counter again. This time, I helped myself to his cereal and to his skim milk, and I even cut up a banana to put on top. It wasn't half bad.

Conrad was turning out to be a pretty good housemate. He always put the seat back down on the toilet, he did his dishes right away, he even bought more paper towels when we ran out. I wouldn't have expected any less, though. Conrad had always been neat. He was the exact opposite of Jeremiah in that way. Jeremiah never changed the roll of toilet paper. It would never occur to him to buy paper towels or to soak a greasy pan in hot water and dishwashing soap.

I went to the grocery store later that day and bought stuff for dinner. Spaghetti and sauce and lettuce and tomato for a salad. I cooked it around seven, thinking, ha! This will show him how healthily I can eat. I ended up overcooking the pasta and not rinsing the lettuce thoroughly enough, but it still tasted fine.

Conrad didn't come home, though, so I ate it alone in front of the TV. I did put some leftovers on a plate for him, though, and I left it on the counter when I went up to bed.

The next morning, it was gone and the dish was washed.

chapter *thirty-one*

The next time Conrad and I spoke to each other, it was the middle of the day and I was sitting at the kitchen table with my wedding binder. Now that we had our guest list, the next thing I needed to do was mail off our invitations. It almost seemed silly to bother with invitations when we had so few guests, but a mass e-mail didn't feel quite right either. I got the invitations from David's Bridal. They were white with light turquoise shells, and all I had to do was run them through the printer. And poof, wedding invitations.

Conrad opened the sliding door and stepped into the kitchen. His gray T-shirt was soaked in sweat, so I guessed he'd gone for a run. "Good run?" I asked him.

"Yeah," he said, looking surprised. He looked at my stack of envelopes and asked, "Wedding invitations?"

"Yup. I just need to go get stamps."

Pouring himself a glass of water, he said, "I need to go into town and get a new drill at the hardware store. The post office is on the way. I can get your stamps."

It was my turn to look surprised. "Thanks," I said, "but I want to go and see what kind of love stamps they have."

He downed his water.

"Do you know what a love stamp is?" I didn't wait for him to answer. "It's a stamp that says 'love' on it. People use them for weddings. I only know because Taylor told me I had to get them."

Conrad half smiled and said, "We can take my car if you want. Save you a trip."

"Sure," I said.

"I'm gonna take a quick shower. Give me ten minutes," he said, and ran up the stairs.

Conrad was back downstairs in ten minutes, just like he said. He grabbed his keys off the counter, I slid my invitations into my purse, and then we headed out to the driveway.

"We can take my car," I offered.

"I don't mind," he said.

It felt sort of funny sitting in the passenger seat of Conrad's car again. His car was clean; it still smelled the same.

"I can't remember the last time I was in your car," I said, turning on the radio.

Without missing a beat, he said, "Your prom."

Oh, God.

Prom. The site of our breakup—us fighting in the

parking lot in the rain. It was embarrassing to think of it now. How I had cried, how I had begged him not to go. Not one of my finest moments.

There was an awkward silence between us, and I had a feeling we were both remembering the same thing. To fill the silence I said brightly, "Gosh, that was, like, a million years ago, huh?"

This time he didn't reply.

Conrad dropped me off in front of the post office and said he'd be back to pick me up in a few minutes. I hopped out of the car and ran inside.

The line moved quickly, and when it was my turn, I said, "Can I see your love stamp, please?"

The woman behind the counter rifled through her drawer and slid a sheet of stamps over to me. They had wedding bells on them and LOVE was inscribed on a ribbon tying the bells together.

I set my stack of invitations on the counter and counted them quickly. "I'll take a sheet," I said.

Eyeing me, she asked, "Are those wedding invitations?"

"Yes," I said.

"Do you want to hand cancel them?"

"Pardon?"

"Do you want to hand cancel them?" she repeated, and this time she sounded annoyed.

I panicked. What did "hand cancel" mean? I wanted to text Taylor and ask, but there was a line growing behind me, so I said hastily, "No, thank you."

After I paid for the stamps, I went outside, sat on the curb, and stamped all my invitations—one for my mother, too. Just in case. She could still change her mind. There was still a chance. Conrad drove up as I was pushing them through the mail slot outside. This was really happening. I was really getting married. No turning back now, not that I wanted to.

Climbing into the car, I asked, "Did you get your new drill?"

"Yep," he said. "Did you find your love stamps?"

"Yep," I said. "Hey, what does it mean to hand cancel mail?"

"Canceling is when the post office marks the stamp so it can't be used again. I guess hand canceling would be doing it by hand instead of machine."

"How did you know that?" I asked, impressed.

"I used to collect stamps."

That was right. He had collected stamps. I'd forgotten. He kept them in a photo album his dad gave him.

"I totally forgot about that. Holy crap, you were so serious about your stamps. You wouldn't even let us touch your book without permission. Remember how Jeremiah stole one and used it to send a postcard and you were so mad you cried?"

"Hey, that was my Abraham Lincoln stamp that my grandpa gave me," Conrad said defensively. "That was a rare stamp."

I laughed, and then he did too. It was a nice sound. When was the last time we'd laughed like this?

Shaking his head, he said, "I was such a little geek."

"No, you weren't!"

Conrad threw me a look. "Stamp collecting. Chemistry set. Encyclopedia obsession."

"Yeah, but you made all of that seem cool," I said. In my memory Conrad was no geek. He was older, smarter, interested in grown-up things.

"You were gullible," he said. And then, "When you were really little, you hated carrots. You wouldn't eat them. But then I told you that if you ate carrots, you'd get X-ray vision. And you believed me. You used to believe everything I said."

I did. I really did.

I believed him when he said that carrots could give me X-ray vision. I believed him when he told me that he'd never cared about me. And then, later that night, when he tried to take it back, I guess I believed him again. Now I didn't know what to believe. I just knew I didn't believe in him anymore.

I changed the subject. Abruptly, I asked, "Are you going to stay in California after you graduate?"

"It depends on med school," he said.

"Are you . . . do you have a girlfriend?"

I saw him start. I saw him hesitate.

"No," he said.

chapter *thirty-two*
CONRAD

Her name was Agnes. A lot of people called her Aggie, but I stuck with Agnes. She was in my chem class. On any other girl, a name like Agnes wouldn't have worked. It was an old-lady name. Agnes had short dirty-blond hair, it was wavy, and she had it cut at her chin. Sometimes she wore glasses, and her skin was as pale as milk. When we were waiting for the lab to open up one day, she asked me out. I was so surprised, I said yes.

We started hanging out a lot. I liked being around her. She was smart, and her hair carried the smell of her shampoo not just fresh out of the shower but for a whole day. We spent most of our time together studying. Sometimes we'd go get pancakes or burgers after, sometimes we'd hook up in her room during a study break when her roommate wasn't around. But it was all centered around both of us being pre-med. It wasn't like I spent the night in her room or invited her to stay over in mine. I didn't hang out with her and her friends or meet her parents, even though they lived nearby.

One day we were studying in the library. The semester was almost over. We'd been dating two, almost three, months.

Out of nowhere, she asked me, "Have you ever been in love?"

Not only was Agnes good at no chem, she was really good at catching me off guard. I looked around to see if anyone was listening. "Have you?"

"I asked you first," she said.

"Then yes."

"How many times?"

"Once."

Agnes absorbed my answer as she chewed on her pencil. "On a scale of one to ten, how in love were you?"

"You can't put being in love on a scale," I said. "Either you are or you aren't."

"But if you had to say."

I started flipping through my notes. I didn't look at her when I said, "Ten."

"Wow. What was her name?"

"Agnes, come on. We have an exam on Friday."

Agnes made a pouty face and kicked my leg under the

table. "If you don't tell me, I won't be able to concentrate. Please? Just humor me."

I let out a short breath. "Belly. I mean, Isabel. Satisfied?"

Shaking her head, she said, "Uh-uh. Now tell me how you met."

"Agnes—"

"I swear I'll stop if you just answer"—I watched her count in her head—"three more questions. Three and that's it."

I didn't say yes or no, I just looked at her, waiting.

"So, how did you meet?"

"We never really met. I just always knew her."

"When did you know you were in love?"

I didn't have an answer to that question. There hadn't been one specific moment. It was like gradually waking up. You go from being asleep to the space between dreaming and awake and then into consciousness. It's a slow process, but when you're awake, there's no mistaking it. There was no mistaking that it had been love.

But I wasn't going to say that to Agnes. "I don't know, it just happened."

She looked at me, waiting for me to go on.

"You have one more question," I said.

"Are you in love with me?"

Like I said, this girl was really good at catching me off guard. I didn't know what to say. Because the answer was no. "Um . . ."

Her face fell, and then she tried to sound upbeat as she said, "So no, huh?"

"Well, are you in love with me?"

"I could be. If I let myself, I think I could be."

"Oh." I felt like a piece of shit. "I really do like you, Agnes."

"I know. I can feel that that's true. You're an honest guy, Conrad. But you don't let people in. It's impossible to get close to you." She tried to put her hair in a pony-tail, but the front pieces kept falling out because it was so short. Then she released her hair and said, "I think you still love that other girl, at least a little bit. Am I right?"

"No," I told Belly.

"I don't believe you," she said, tilting her head to one side. Teasingly, she said, "If there wasn't a girl, why would you stay away for so long? There has to be a girl."

There was.

I'd stayed away for two years. I had to. I knew I shouldn't even be at the summer house, because being there, being near her, I would just want what I couldn't have. It was dangerous. She was the one person I didn't trust myself around. The day she showed up with Jere, I called my friend Danny to see if I could crash on his couch for a while, and he'd said yes. But I couldn't bring myself to do it. I couldn't leave.

I knew I had to be careful. I had to keep my distance.

If she knew how much I still cared, it was all over. I wouldn't be able to walk away again. The first time was hard enough.

The promises you make on your mother's deathbed are promises that are absolute; they're titanium. There's no way you're breaking them. I promised my mother that I would take care of my brother. That I would look after him. I kept my word. I did it the best way I could. By leaving.

I might have been a fuckup and a failure and a disappointment, but I wasn't a liar.

I did lie to Belly, though. Just that one time in that crappy motel. I did it to protect her. That's what I kept telling myself. Still, if there was one moment in my life I could redo, one moment out of all the shitty moments, that was the one I'd pick. When I thought back to the look on her face—the way it just crumpled, how she'd sucked in her lips and wrinkled her nose to keep the hurt from showing—it killed me. God, if I could, I'd go back to that moment and say all the right things, I'd tell her I loved her, I'd make it so that she never looked that way again.

chapter *thirty-three*
CONRAD

That night in the motel, I didn't sleep. I went over and over everything that had ever happened between us. I couldn't keep doing it, going back and forth, holding her close and then pushing her away. It wasn't right.

When Belly got up to shower around dawn, Jere and I got up too. I was folding my blanket up when I said, "It's okay if you like her."

Jere stared at me, his mouth hanging open. "What are you talking about?"

I felt like I was choking as I said, "It's okay with me . . . if you want to be with her."

He looked at me like I was crazy. I felt like I'd gone crazy. I heard the water in the shower shut off, and I turned away from him and said, "Just take care of her."

And then, when she came out, dressed, her hair wet,

she looked at me with those hopeful eyes, and I looked back at her like I didn't recognize her. Completely blank. I saw her eyes dim. I saw her love for me die. I'd killed it.

When I thought about it now, that moment in the motel, I understood I was the one who'd set this thing in motion. Pushed them together. It was my doing. I was the one who was going to have to live with it. They were happy.

I'd been doing a pretty good job of making myself scarce, but I happened to be home that Friday afternoon when, out of nowhere, Belly needed me. She was sitting on the living room floor with that stupid binder, papers all around her. She looked freaked out, stressed. She had that worried grimace on her face, the look she'd get when she was working on a math problem and she couldn't figure it out.

"Jere's stuck in city traffic," she said, blowing her hair out of her face. "I told him to leave earlier. I really needed his help today."

"What did you need him to do?"

"We were gonna go to Michaels. You know, that craft store?"

Drily, I said, "I can't say I've ever been to a Michaels before." I hesitated, then added, "But if you want, I'll go with you."

"Really? Because I'm picking up some heavy stuff today. The store's all the way over in Plymouth, though."

"Sure, no problem," I said, feeling inexplicably gratified to be lifting heavy stuff.

We took her car because it was bigger. She drove. I'd only ever ridden with her a few times. This side of her was new to me. Assured, confident. She drove fast, but she was still in control. I liked it. I found myself sneaking peeks at her, and I had to force myself to cool it.

"You're not a bad driver," I said.

She grinned. "Jeremiah taught me well."

That's right. He taught her how to drive. "So what else about you has changed?"

"Hey, I was never not a good driver."

I snorted, then looked out the window. "I think Steve would disagree."

"He'll never let me live down what I did to his precious baby." She shifted gears as we came to a stoplight. "So what else?"

"You wear heels now. At the garden ceremony, you had on high heels."

There was a minute hesitation before she said, "Yeah, sometimes. I still trip in them, though." Ruefully she added, "I'm like a real lady now."

I reached out to touch her hand, but at the last second I pointed instead. "You still bite your nails."

She curled her fingers around the steering wheel. With a little smile, she said, "You don't miss a thing."

"Okay, so, what are we picking up here? Flower holders?"

Belly laughed. "Yeah. Flower holders. In other words, vases." She grabbed a cart, and I took it from her and pushed it in front of us. "I think we decided on hurricane vases."

"What's a hurricane vase? And how the hell does Jere know what one is?"

"I didn't mean Jere and I decided, I meant me and Taylor." She grabbed the cart and walked ahead of me. I followed her to aisle twelve.

"See?" Belly held up a fat glass vase.

I crossed my arms. "Very nice," I said in a bored voice.

She put down the vase and picked up a skinnier one, and she didn't look at me as she said, "I'm sorry you're the one stuck doing this with me. I know it's lame."

"It's not—that lame," I said. I started grabbing vases off the shelf. "How many do we need?"

"Wait! Should we get the big ones or the medium ones? I'm thinking maybe the medium ones," she said, lifting one up and checking the price tag. "Yeah, definitely the medium ones. I only see a few left. Can you go ask somebody who works here?"

"The big ones," I said, because I'd already stacked four of the big ones in the cart. "The big ones are much nicer. You can fit more flowers or sand or whatever."

Belly narrowed her eyes. "You're just saying that because you don't want to go find somebody."

"Okay, yeah, but seriously, I think the big ones are nicer."

She shrugged and put another big vase in the cart. "I guess we could just have one big vase on each table instead of two medium-size ones."

"Now what?" I started to push the cart again, and she took it from me.

"Candles."

I followed her down another aisle, then another. "I don't think you know where you're going," I said.

"I'm taking you on the scenic route," she said, steering the cart. "Look at all these fake flowers and garlands. Good stuff."

I stopped. "Should we get some? They might look good on the porch." I grabbed a bunch of sunflowers and added a few white roses to the bunch. "This looks kind of nice, right?"

"I was kidding," she said, sucking in her cheeks. I could tell she was trying not to smile. "But yeah, that looks all right. Not great, but all right."

I put the flowers back. "All right, I give up. From now on, I'll just do the heavy lifting."

"Nice effort, though."

Back at the house, Jeremiah's car was in the driveway.

"Jere and I can unload all of this later," I said, turning off the ignition.

"I'll help," she offered, hopping out of the car. "I'm just gonna say hi first."

I grabbed a couple of the heavier bags and followed her up the steps and into the house. Jeremiah was lying on the couch watching TV. When he saw us, he sat up. "Where have you guys been?" he asked. He said it casually, but his eyes flickered at me as he spoke.

"At Michaels," Belly said. "What time did you get here?"

"A little while ago. Why didn't you wait for me? I told you I'd be here in time." Jeremiah got up and crossed the room. He pulled Belly toward him for a hug.

"I told you, Michaels closes at nine. I doubt you would have made it in time," she said, and she sounded pissed, but she let him kiss her.

I turned away. "I'm gonna go unload the car."

"Wait, I'll help." Jeremiah released Belly and slapped his hand on my back. "Con, thanks for pinch-hitting for me today."

"No problem."

"It's after eight," Belly said. "I'm starving. Let's all go to Jimmy's for dinner."

I shook my head. "Nah, I'm not hungry. You guys go."

"But you didn't have any dinner," Belly said, frowning. "Just come with us."

"No, thanks," I said.

She started to protest again, but Jere said, "Bells, he doesn't want to. Let's just go."

"Are you sure?" she asked me.

"I'm good," I said, and it came out harsher than I meant it.

I guessed it worked though, because they left.

chapter *thirty-four*

At Jimmy's, neither of us ordered crabs. I got fried scallops and iced tea, and Jeremiah got a lobster roll and beer. The server asked for his ID and smirked when he saw it, but he still served him a beer.

I shook a few sugar packets into my iced tea, tasted it, then added two more.

"I'm wiped," Jeremiah said, leaning back into the booth and closing his eyes.

"Well, wake up. We have work to do."

He opened his eyes. "Like what?"

"What do you mean, like what? Tons of stuff. At David's Bridal they were asking me all these questions. Like, what's our color palette? And are you going to wear a suit or a tuxedo?"

Jeremiah snorted. "A tuxedo? On the beach? I probably won't even wear shoes."

"Well, yeah, I know, but you should probably figure out what you're going to wear."

"I don't know. You tell me. I'll wear whatever you and Taylor want me to wear. It's your guys's day, right?"

"Ha ha," I said. "Very funny." It wasn't like I really cared what he wore. I just wanted him to figure it out and let me know so I could check it off my list.

Drumming his fingers on the table, he said, "I was thinking white shirts and khaki shorts. Nice and simple, like we said."

"Okay."

Jeremiah gulped his beer. "Hey, can we dance to 'You Never Can Tell' at the reception?"

"I don't know that song," I said.

"Sure you do. It's from my favorite movie. Hint: we had the soundtrack on repeat in our frat house media room all semester." When I still stared at him blankly, Jeremiah sang, "It was a teenage wedding and the old folks wished them well."

"Oh, yeah. *Pulp Fiction.*"

"So can we?"

"Are you serious?"

"Come on, Bells. Be a sport. We can put it on YouTube. I bet we'll get a shit ton of hits. It'll be funny!"

I gave him a look. "Funny? You want our wedding to be funny?"

"Come on. You're making all the decisions, and all I

want is this one thing," he said, pouting, and I couldn't tell if he was serious or not. Either way, it pissed me off. Plus, I was still pissed he hadn't made it in time to help me at Michaels.

The server came by with our food, and Jeremiah dug right in to his lobster roll.

"What other decisions have I made?" I asked him.

"You decided that the cake was going to be carrot," he reminded me, mayonnaise dripping down his chin. "I like chocolate cake."

"I don't want to be the one making all the decisions! I don't even know what I'm doing."

"Then I'll help more. Just tell me what to do. Hey, I've got an idea. What if the wedding was Tarantino themed?" he said.

"Yeah, what if," I said sourly. I stabbed a scallop with my fork.

"You could be the Bride like in *Kill Bill*." He looked up from his plate. "Kidding, kidding. But this whole thing is still gonna be pretty chill, right? We said we just wanted it to be casual."

"Yeah, but people still need to, like, eat."

"Don't worry about the food and stuff. My dad will hire somebody to take care of all that."

I could feel irritation start to prickle beneath my skin like a heat rash. I let out a short breath. "It's easy for you to say don't worry. You're not the one planning our wedding."

Jeremiah put down his sandwich and sat up straight. "I told you I'd help. And like I said, my dad will take care of a lot of it."

"I don't want him to," I said. "I want us to do it together. And joking about Quent Tarantino movies doesn't really count as helping."

"It's Quent*in*," Jeremiah corrected.

I shot him a dirty look.

"I wasn't joking about the first dance," he said. "I still think it would be cool. And Bells, I have been doing stuff. I figured out what to do for music. My buddy Pete dee-jays on the weekends. He said he'd bring his speakers and just hook up his iPod and take care of the whole thing. He already has the *Pulp Fiction* soundtrack, by the way."

Jeremiah raised his eyebrows at me comically. I knew he was waiting for a laugh or at least a smile. And I was about to give in, just so this fight could be over and I could eat my scallops without feeling angry, when he said innocently, "Oh, wait, did you want to check with Taylor first? See if she'd be okay with it?"

I glared at him. He needed to quit with the jokes and start acting a lot more appreciative, because Taylor was the one who was actually helping, unlike him. "I don't need to check with her on this. It's a dumb idea, and it's not happening."

Jeremiah whistled under his breath. "All righty, Bridezilla."

"I'm not a Bridezilla! I don't even want to do any of this. *You* do it."

He stared at me. "What do you mean, you don't want to do any of this?"

My heart was beating really fast all of a sudden. "I mean the planning. I don't want to do any of this stupid planning. Not the actual getting married part. I still want to do that."

"Good. Me too." He reached across the table, plucked a scallop off my plate, and popped it into his mouth.

I stuffed the last scallop into my mouth before he could take that, too. Then I grabbed a bunch of fries off of his plate, even though I had fries of my own.

"Hey," he said with a frown. "You've got your own fries."

"Yours are crispier," I said, but really it was more out of spite. I wondered—the rest of our lives, was Jeremiah going to try and eat my last scallop or my last bite of steak? I liked finishing all the food on my plate—I wasn't one of those girls who left a few bites behind just to be polite.

I had a fry in my mouth when Jeremiah asked, "Has Laurel called at all?"

I swallowed. Suddenly I wasn't so hungry anymore. "No."

"She must have gotten the invite by now."

"Yeah."

"Well, hopefully she'll call this week," Jere said, stuffing the rest of his lobster roll into his mouth. "I mean, I'm sure she will."

"Hopefully," I said. I sipped on my iced tea and added, "Our first dance can be 'You Never Can Tell' if you really want."

Jere pumped his fist in the air. "See, that's why I'm marrying you!"

A smile creeped across my face. "Because I'm generous?"

"Because you're very generous, and you get me," he said, taking back a few of his fries.

When we got back to the house, Conrad's car was gone.

chapter *thirty-five*
CONRAD

I would rather have had someone shoot me in the head with a nail gun, repeatedly, than have to watch the two of them cuddling on the couch together all night. After they went to dinner, I got in my car and drove to Boston. As I drove, I thought about not going back to Cousins. Screw it. It would be easier that way. Halfway home, I made up my mind that yeah, that would be for the best. An hour from home, I decided, screw them, I had as much right to be there as they did. I still needed to clean out the gutters, and I was pretty sure I'd seen a wasp nest in the drainpipe. There was all kinds of stuff I needed to take care of. I couldn't just not go back.

Around midnight, I was sitting at the kitchen table in my boxer shorts eating cereal when my dad walked in, still wearing his work suit. I didn't even know he was home.

He didn't look surprised to see me. "Con, can I talk to you for a minute?" he asked.

"Yeah."

He sat down across from me with his glass of bourbon. In the dim light of the kitchen, my father looked like an old man. His hair was thinning on top, and he'd lost weight, too much weight. When did he get so old? In my mind he was always thirty-seven.

My dad cleared his throat. "What do you think I should do about this thing with Jeremiah? I mean, is he really set on it?"

"Yeah, I think he is."

"Laurel's really torn up about it. She's tried everything, but the kids aren't listening. Belly ran off, and now they aren't even talking to each other. You know how Laurel can get."

This was all news to me. I didn't know they weren't speaking to each other.

My dad sipped from his glass. "Do you think there's anything I can do? To put an end to it?"

For once I actually agreed with my dad. My feelings for Belly aside, I thought getting married at nineteen was dumb. What was the point? What were they trying to prove?

"You could cut Jere off," I said, and then I felt like a dick for suggesting it. I added, "But even if you did, he still has the money Mom left him."

"Most of it's in a trust."

"He's determined. He'll do it either way." I hesitated, then added, "Besides, if you pulled something like that, he'd never forgive you."

My dad got up and poured himself some more bourbon. He sipped it before he said, "I don't want to lose him the way I lost you."

I didn't know what to say. So we sat there in silence, and right when I finally opened my mouth to say, You haven't lost me, he stood up.

Sighing heavily, he emptied his glass. "Good night, son."

"Good night, Dad."

I watched my father trudge up the stairs, each step heavier than the last—like Atlas with the world on his shoulders. He'd never had to deal with this kind of thing before. He'd never had to be that kind of father. My mom was always there to take care of the hard stuff. Now that she was gone, he was all we had left, and it wasn't enough.

I had always been the favorite. I was our father's Jacob, and Jeremiah was Esau. It wasn't something I'd ever questioned; I'd always assumed it was because I was the firstborn that I came first with my dad. I just accepted it, and so did Jere. But as we got older, I saw that that wasn't it. It was that he saw himself in me. To our father, I was just a reflection of him. He thought we were so alike. Jere was like our mom, I was like our dad. So I was the one he put all the pressure on. I was the one he funneled all his energy and hope into. Football, school, all of it. I worked hard to meet those expectations, to be just like him.

The first time I realized my father wasn't perfect was when he forgot my mom's birthday. He'd been golfing all day with his friends, and he came home late. Jere and I had made a cake and bought flowers and a card. We had everything set up on the dining room table. My dad had had a few beers—I could smell it on him when he hugged me. He said, "Oh shit, I forgot. Boys, can I put my name on the card?" I was a freshman in high school. Late, I know, to figure out your dad isn't a hero. That was just the first time I remember being disappointed by something he did. After that, I found more and more reasons to be disappointed.

All of that love and pride I had in him, it turned to hate. And then I started to hate myself, who he'd made. Because I saw it too—how alike we were. That scared me. I didn't want to be the kind of man who cheated on his wife. I didn't want to be the kind of man who put work before his family, who tipped cheaply at restaurants, who never bothered to learn our housekeeper's name.

From there on I set out to destroy the picture of me he had in his head. I quit our morning runs before he left for work, I quit the fishing trips, the golf, which I'd never liked anyway. And I quit football, which I loved. He'd gone to all my games, videotaping them so we could watch later and he could point out the places where I'd messed up. Every time there was an article about me in the newspaper, he framed it and hung it in his study.

I quit it all to spite him. Anything that made him proud of me, I took away.

It took me a long time to figure it out. That I was the one who had put my dad on that pedestal. I did that, not him. And then I despised him for not being perfect. For being human.

I drove back to Cousins on Monday morning.

chapter *thirty-six*

On Monday afternoon Conrad and I were eating outside
on the deck. He had grilled chicken and corn for lunch.
He hadn't been kidding when he said all he ever ate was
grilled chicken.

"Did Jere tell you what he wants you and Steven to
wear for the wedding?" I asked him.

Conrad shook his head, looking confused. "I thought
guys just wore suits for weddings."

"Well, yeah, but you guys are his best men, so you're all
dressing alike. Khaki shorts and white-linen button-down
shirts. He didn't tell you?"

"This is the first I'm hearing about linen shirts. Or
being a best man."

I rolled my eyes. "Jeremiah needs to get on the ball.
Of course you're his best man. You and Steven both are."

"How can there be two best men? 'Best' implies only one." Biting into his corn on the cob, he said, "Let Steven be it, I don't care."

"No! You're Jeremiah's brother. You have to be his best man."

My phone rang as I was explaining to him what being the best man entailed. I didn't recognize the number, but since the wedding planning had gotten under way, I'd been getting a lot of those.

"Is this Isabel?" I didn't recognize the voice. She sounded older, like someone my mother's age. Whoever she was, she had a thick Boston accent.

I said, "Um, this is she. I mean, her."

"My name is Denise Coletti, I'm calling from Adam Fisher's office."

"Oh . . . hello. It's nice to meet you."

"Yes, hello. I just need you to okay a few things for your wedding. I've selected a catering service called Elegantly Yours; they do events around the area. They're doing this very last-minute for us; this caterer books months in advance for parties. Is this all right with you?"

Faintly, I said, "Sure."

Conrad looked at me quizzically, and I mouthed, *Denise Coletti*. His eyes widened, and he gestured for me to give him the phone. I waved his hand away.

Then Denise Coletti said, "Now, how many people are you expecting?"

"Twenty, if everyone can come."

"Adam told me more like forty. I'll check with him." I could hear her typing. "So probably four to five appetizers a person. Do we want a vegetarian option for the meal?"

"I don't think Jeremiah and I have any vegetarian friends."

"All right. Are you going to want to go and do a tasting? I think you probably should."

"Uh, okay."

"Wonderful. I'll book you for next week, then. Now for seating arrangements. Do you want two or three long tables or five round tables?"

"Um . . ." I hadn't even thought of tables. And what was she talking about, forty? I was wishing I had Taylor next to me to tell me what to do. "Can I get back to you on that?"

Denise let out a little sigh, and I knew I had said the wrong thing. "Sure, but be as quick as you can so I can give them the go-ahead. That's all for now. I'll be touching base with you again later this week. Oh, and congratulations."

"Thank you very much, Denise."

Next to me, Conrad called out, "Hi, Denise!"

She said, "Is that Connie? Tell him hello from me."

"Denise says hello," I told him.

Then she said mazel tov, and we hung up.

"What's going on?" Conrad asked me. He had a corn kernel stuck on his cheek. "Why is Denise calling you?"

I put my phone down and said, "Um, apparently, your

dad's secretary is our wedding planner now. And we're inviting forty people instead of twenty."

Blandly, he said, "That's good news."

"How is that good news?"

"It means my dad is okay with you guys getting married. And he's paying for it." Conrad started to cut his chicken.

"Huh. Wow." I stood up. "I'd better call Jere. Wait, it's the middle of the day. He's still at work."

I sat back down.

I probably should have felt relieved that someone else was taking over, but instead I just felt overwhelmed. This wedding was getting a lot bigger than I had imagined it. Now we were renting tables? It was all too much, too sudden.

Across from me, Conrad was buttering another ear of corn. I looked down at my plate. I wasn't hungry anymore. I felt sick to my stomach.

"Eat," Conrad said.

I took a small bite of chicken.

I wouldn't get to talk to Jeremiah until later that evening. But the person I really wanted to talk to was my mother. She would have known how to configure the tables and where to seat everyone. Denise wasn't the one I wanted to swoop in and tell me what to do, and not Mr. Fisher either, or even Susannah. I only wanted my mother.

chapter *thirty-seven*
CONRAD

It didn't really hit me how hard of a time Belly was having until I heard her on the phone with Taylor later that
week. She had her door open, and I was brushing my
teeth in the hall bathroom.

I heard her say, "Taylor, I really appreciate what your
mom is trying to do, but I promise you, it's okay. . . . I
know, but it would just feel too weird with all the adults
from the neighborhood at my wedding shower and then
my mom not being there. . . ." I heard her sigh and say,
"Yeah, I know. Okay. Tell your mom thanks."

She closed her door then, and I was pretty sure I heard
her start to cry.

I went to my room, lay down on my bed, and stared
up at the ceiling.

Belly hadn't let on to me how sad she was about her

mom. She was an upbeat kind of person, naturally cheerful, like Jere. If there was a bright side, Belly would find it. Hearing her cry, it shook me up. I knew I should stay out of it. That was the smart thing to do. She didn't need me looking out for her. She was a big girl. Besides, what could I do for her?

I was definitely staying out of it.

The next morning, I got up early to see Laurel. It was still dark out when I left. I called her on the way and asked if she could meet for breakfast. Laurel was surprised, but she didn't ask questions; she said she'd meet me at a diner off the highway.

I guess Laurel had always been special to me. Ever since I was a kid, I just liked being near her. I liked the way you could be quiet around her, and with her. She didn't talk down to kids. She treated us like equals. After my mom died and I transferred to Stanford, I started calling Laurel every once in a while. I still liked talking to her, and I liked that she reminded me of my mom without it hurting too much. It was like a link to home.

She got to the diner first—she was sitting in a booth waiting for me. "Connie," she said, standing up and opening her arms. She looked like she'd lost weight.

"Hey, Laur," I said, hugging her back. She felt gaunt in my arms, but she smelled the same. Laurel always had a clean, cinnamony smell.

I sat down across from her. After we ordered, pancakes and bacon for both of us, she said, "So how have you been?"

"I've been all right," I said, chugging down some juice.

How was I even supposed to broach this subject? This wasn't my style. It didn't come naturally to me, the way it would for Jere. I was butting in on something that wasn't my business. But I had to do it. For her.

I cleared my throat and said, "I called you because I wanted to talk about the wedding."

Her face got tight, but she didn't interrupt.

"Laur, I think you should go. I think you should be part of it. You're her mom."

Laurel stirred her coffee, and then she looked at me and said, "You think they should get married?"

"I didn't say that."

"Then, what do you think?"

"I think they love each other and they're going to do it regardless of what anyone else thinks. And . . . I think that Belly really needs her mom right now."

Drily, she said, "Isabel seems to be doing just fine without me. She never even called to let me know where she was. I had to hear it from Adam—who, by the way, is apparently paying for this wedding now. Classic Adam. And now Steven's a best man, and Belly's dad is going to give in the way he always does. It seems I'm the only holdout."

"Belly isn't fine. She's barely eating. And . . . I heard her crying last night. She was saying how Taylor's mom is throwing her a wedding shower but it won't feel right without you there."

Laurel's face softened, just a little. "Lucinda's throwing her a shower?" Then, stirring her coffee again, she said, "Jere hasn't thought this through. He isn't taking it seriously enough."

"You're right, he's not a serious guy. But believe me, he's serious about her." I took a deep breath before I said, "Laurel, if you don't go, you'll regret it."

She looked at me directly. "Are we speaking honestly with each other here?"

"Don't we always?"

Laurel nodded, taking a sip of coffee. "Yes, that we do. So tell me. What's your interest in all of this?"

I knew this was coming. This was Laurel, after all. She didn't mess around. "I want her to be happy."

"Ah," she said. "Just her?"

"Jeremiah, too."

"And that's it?" She looked at me steadily.

I just looked back at her.

I tried to pay for breakfast since I was the one who invited her out, but Laurel wouldn't let me. "Not gonna happen," she said.

On the drive back, I played back our conversation. The

knowing look on Laur's face when she asked me what my interest in this was. What was I doing? Picking out vases with Belly, trying to play peacemaker with the parents. Suddenly I was their wedding planner, and I didn't even agree with them. I needed to disengage from the situation. I was washing my hands of the whole mess.

chapter *thirty-eight*

"Where have you been?" I asked Conrad when he came back in the door. He'd been gone all morning.

He didn't answer me right away. In fact he was barely looking at me. And then he said, shortly, "Just running errands."

I gave him a weird look, but he didn't offer up any more information. So I just asked, "Wanna keep me company while I go to the florist in Dyerstown? I have to pick out flowers for the wedding."

"Isn't Jere coming today? Can't you go with him?" He sounded annoyed.

I was surprised and a little hurt. I thought we'd been getting along really well these past few weeks. "He's not going to be here until tonight," I said. Playfully, I added, "Anyway, you're the one who's the flower-arranging expert, not Jere, remember?"

Conrad stood at the sink with his back to me. He turned on the water, filling a glass. "I don't want to piss him off."

I thought I heard a trace of hurt in his voice. Hurt—and something else. Fear.

"What's wrong? Did something happen this morning?" I felt worried all of a sudden. When Conrad didn't answer me, I went up behind him and started to put my hand on his shoulder, but then he turned around and my hand fell back to my side. "Nothing happened," he said. "Let's go. I'll drive."

He was pretty quiet at the florist's. Taylor and I had decided on calla lilies, but when I looked through the book of flower arrangements, I ended up picking peonies instead. When I showed them to Conrad, he said, "Those were my mom's favorite."

"I remember," I said. I ordered five arrangements, one for each table, just like Denise Coletti told me to.

"What about bouquets?" the florist asked me.

"Can those be peonies too?" I asked.

"Sure, we can do that. I'll put together something nice for you." To Conrad, she said, "Are you and your groomsmen doing boutonnieres?"

He turned red. "I'm not the groom," he said.

"He's the brother of the groom," I said, handing her Mr. Fisher's credit card.

We left pretty soon after.

On the way back home, we passed a fruit stand on the side of the road. I wanted to stop, but I didn't say so. I guessed Conrad could tell, because he asked, "Want to go back?"

"Nah, that's okay, we already passed it," I said.

He made a U-turn on the one-way street.

The fruit stand was a couple of wooden crates of peaches and a sign that said to leave the money in the container. I put in a dollar because I didn't have change.

"Aren't you going to have one?" I asked him, wiping off my peach on my shirt.

"Nah, I'm allergic to peaches."

"Since when?" I demanded. "I've definitely seen you eat a peach before. Or peach pie, at least."

He shrugged. "Since always. I've eaten them before, but they make the inside of my mouth itch."

Before I bit into my peach, I closed my eyes and inhaled the fragrance. "Your loss."

I had never had a peach like that before. So perfectly ripe. Your fingers sank into the fruit a little just touching it. I gobbled it up, peach juice running down my chin, pulp dripping all over my hands. It was sweet and tart. A full-body experience, smell and taste and sight.

"This is a perfect peach," I said. "I almost don't want to have another one, because there's no way it can be as good."

"Let's test it out," Conrad said, and he went and

bought me another peach. I ate that one in four bites.

"Was it as good?" he asked me.

"Yeah. It was."

Conrad reached out and wiped my chin with his shirt. It was maybe the most intimate thing anyone had ever done to me.

I felt light-headed, unsteady on my feet.

It was all in the way he looked at me, just those few seconds. Then he dropped his eyes, like the sun was too bright behind me.

I sidestepped away from him and said, "I'm gonna buy some more, for Jere."

"Good idea," he said, backing away. "I'll go wait for you in the car."

I was shaking as I piled peaches into a plastic bag. Just one look, one touch from him, and I was shaking. It was madness. I was marrying his brother.

Back in the car, I didn't speak. I couldn't have even if I wanted to. I didn't have the words. In the quiet of the air-conditioned car, the silence between us felt blaringly loud. So I rolled down my window and fixed my eyes on all the moving objects on my side.

At home, Jeremiah's car was parked in the driveway. Conrad disappeared as soon as we got into the house. I found Jere napping on the couch, his sunglasses still on his head. I kissed him awake.

His eyes fluttered open. "Hey."

"Hey. Want a peach?" I asked, swinging my plastic bag like a pendulum. I felt jittery all of a sudden.

Jere hugged me and said, "You're a peach."

"Did you know Conrad's allergic to peaches?"

"Of course. Remember that time he had peach ice cream and his mouth swelled up?"

I broke away and went to wash the peaches. I told myself, there's nothing to feel guilty about, nothing happened. You didn't do anything.

I was rinsing peaches in the red plastic colander, shaking excess water off the way I'd seen Susannah do so many times. While the water was running over the peaches, Jeremiah came up behind me and grabbed one, saying, "I think they're clean now."

He lifted himself onto the kitchen counter and bit into the peach.

"Good, right?" I asked him. I held one up to my face and inhaled deeply, trying to clear my mind of all the crazy thoughts.

Jeremiah nodded. He'd already finished it and was lobbing the pit into the sink. "Really good. Did you get any strawberries? I could eat a whole box of strawberries right now."

"No, just the peaches."

I put the peaches in the silver fruit bowl, arranging them as nicely as I could. My hands were still shaking.

chapter *thirty-nine*

The apartment had wall-to-wall navy blue carpeting, and even though I had flip-flops on, I could just tell that it was moist. The kitchen was the size of an airplane bathroom, practically, and the bedroom had no windows. The place had high ceilings—that was the only nice thing about it, in my opinion.

Jeremiah and I had spent the whole day looking at apartments near our school. So far we'd seen three. This place was the worst by far.

"I like the carpet," Jeremiah said appreciatively. "It's nice to wake up in the morning and put your feet down on carpet."

I glanced toward the open door, where the landlord was waiting for us. He looked around my dad's age. He had a long white ponytail, a mustache, and a tattoo of a topless mermaid on his forearm. He caught me looking at the tattoo and grinned at me. I gave him a weak smile in return.

Then I walked back into the bedroom and motioned for Jeremiah to follow me. "It smells like cigarette smoke in here," I whispered. "It's, like, absorbed in the carpet."

"Febreeze it, baby."

"*You* Febreeze it. By yourself. I'm not living here."

"What's the problem? This place is practically on campus, it's so close. And there's outdoor space—we can grill. Think of all the parties we'll have. Come on, Belly."

"Come on nothing. Let's go back to the first place we looked at. That place had central air-conditioning." Above us, I could feel rather than hear the bass from someone's stereo pumping.

Jeremiah jammed his hands into his pockets. "That place was all old people and families. This place is for people our age. College kids like us."

I looked back at the landlord. He was looking at his cell phone, pretending not to listen to our conversation.

Lowering my voice, I said, "This place is basically a frat house. If I wanted to live in a frat house, I would bunk with you back at fraternity row."

He rolled his eyes. Loudly, he said, "I guess we're not taking the apartment." To the landlord, he shrugged, like whaddyagonnado. Like they were in on it together, just a couple of guys, partners.

"Thank you for showing us the apartment," I said.

"No problemo," the guy said, lighting a cigarette.

As we stepped out of the apartment, I shot Jeremiah a dirty look. He mouthed, *What*, in a bewildered way. I just shook my head.

"It's getting late," Jeremiah said in the car. "Let's just pick a place. I want to get this over with already."

"Okay, fine," I said, turning up the AC. "Then I pick the first place."

"Fine," he said.

"Fine," I said back.

We went back to the first apartment complex to fill out paperwork. We went straight to the management office. The building manager's name was Carolyn. She was tall and red haired and she wore a printed wrap dress. Her perfume smelled like Susannah's. I took this as a definite good omen.

"So your parents aren't renting the apartment for you?" Carolyn asked. "Most students have their parents sign the lease."

I opened my mouth to speak, but Jeremiah beat me to it.

"No, we're doing this on our own," he said. "We're engaged."

Surprise registered on her face, and I saw her glance ever so briefly at my stomach. "Oh!" she said. "Well, congratulations."

"Thank you," Jeremiah said.

I said nothing. Inside, I was thinking how sick I was of everybody thinking I was pregnant just because we were getting married.

"We'll need to do a credit check, and then I can process your application," Carolyn said. "If everything checks out, the apartment is yours."

"If you've been late on a few credit-card bills, will that, um, negatively impact a person's credit?" Jeremiah asked, leaning forward.

I could feel my eyes widen. "What are you talking about?" I whispered. "Your dad pays your credit card."

"Yeah, I know, but I started one freshman year too. To build my credit," he added, giving Carolyn a winning smile.

"I'm sure it'll be fine," she said, but her smile had faded. "Isabel, how's your credit?"

"Um, good, I think. My dad put me down on his credit card, but I never use it," I said.

"Hmm. Okay, how about any department-store cards?" she asked.

I shook my head.

"We definitely have first and last month's rent," Jeremiah put in. "And we have the security deposit, too. So it's all good."

"Great," Carolyn said, and she stood up from her chair. "I'm going to process this today, and I'll let you guys know within the next couple of days."

"I'll keep my fingers crossed," I said, trying to sound cheerful.

Jeremiah and I walked out of the building and to the parking lot. When we were standing outside the car, I said, "I really hope we get that apartment."

"If we don't, I'm sure we can get one of the other ones. I doubt Gary would even do a credit check on us."

"Who's Gary?"

Jeremiah went around to the driver's side and unlocked the door. "That guy from the last apartment we saw."

I rolled my eyes. "I'm sure Gary would still do a credit check."

"Doubt it," Jere said. "Gary was cool."

"*Gary* probably has a meth lab in the basement," I said, and this time Jeremiah rolled his eyes.

I continued. "If we lived in that apartment, we would probably wake up in the middle of the night in an ice bath without our kidneys."

"Belly, he rents apartments to lots of students. A guy from my soccer team lived there all last year, and he's fine. Still has both kidneys and everything."

We looked at each other from across the car, on opposite sides. Jere said, "Why are we still talking about this? You got your way, remember?"

He didn't finish the sentence the way I knew he

wanted to—You got your way, like you always do.

"We don't know if I got my way or not."

I didn't finish the sentence the way I wanted to—We don't know if I got my way or not, because of your bad credit.

I jerked the passenger door open and got in.

I got the call later that week. We didn't get the apartment. I didn't know if it was because of Jere's bad credit or my lack of credit, but who really cared. The point was, we didn't get it.

chapter *forty*

It was the day of Taylor's bridal shower. I kept thinking of it as her shower because she and her mom were the ones who were throwing it. The invitations they sent out were nicer than my actual wedding invitations.

There were already a bunch of cars parked in front of the house. I recognized Marcy Yoo's silver Audi and Taylor's Aunt Mindy's blue Honda. Taylor's mailbox had white balloons strung on it. It reminded me of every birthday party Taylor had ever had. She always had hot pink balloons. Always.

I was wearing a white sundress and sandals. I'd put on mascara and blush and pink lip gloss. When I'd left the Cousins house, Conrad said I looked nice. It was the first time we'd spoken since the day we stopped for peaches. He said, *You look nice*, and I said thanks. Totally normal.

I rang the doorbell, something I never did at Taylor's house. But since it was a party, I figured I should.

Taylor answered the door. She was wearing a pink dress with light green fish swimming along the hem, and she'd done her hair halfway up. She looked like she should be the bride, not me. "You look pretty," she said, hugging me.

"So do you," I said, stepping inside.

"Almost everybody's here," she said, leading me to the living room.

"I'm just gonna go pee first," I said.

"Hurry, you're the guest of honor."

I used the bathroom quickly, and after I washed my hands, I tried to brush my hair with my fingers. I put a little more lip gloss on. For some reason, I felt nervous.

Taylor had hung crepe-paper wedding bells from the ceiling, and "Going to the Chapel" was playing on the stereo.

There were our friends Marcy and Blair and Katie, Taylor's Aunt Mindy, my next door-neighbor Mrs. Evans, Taylor's mom Lucinda. And sitting next to her, on the loveseat, wearing a light blue suit, was my mother.

My eyes filled when I saw her.

We didn't run across the room to embrace, we didn't weep. I made my way around the room, hugging women and girls, and when I finally reached my mother, we hugged tightly and for a long time. We didn't have to say anything, because we both knew.

At the buffet table, Taylor squeezed my hand. "Happy?" she whispered.

"So happy," I whispered back, picking up a plate. I felt such immense relief. Everything was really working out. I had my mom back. This was really happening.

"Good," Taylor said.

"How did this even happen? Did your mom talk to my mom?"

"Mm-hmm," she said, and she blew me a little kiss. "My mom said it wasn't even hard to convince her to come."

Lucinda had set up the table with her famous white coconut cake as the centerpiece. There was sparkling lemonade, pigs in a blanket, baby carrots, and onion dip— all my favorite foods. My mom had brought her lemon squares.

I filled my plate with food and sat next to the girls. Popping a pig in a blanket in my mouth, I said, "Thank you guys so much for coming!"

"I can't believe you're getting married," Marcy said, shaking her head in awe.

"Me either," Blair said.

"Me either," I said.

Opening presents was the best part. It felt like my birthday. Cupcake tins from Marcy, drinking glasses from Blair, hand towels from Aunt Mindy, cookbooks from Lucinda, a glass pitcher from Taylor, a down comforter from my mother.

Taylor sat next to me, writing down who gave what and collecting ribbons. She poked holes into a paper plate and wove the ribbons through.

"What's that for?" I asked her.

"Your bouquet for the rehearsal, silly," Lucinda said, beaming at me. She'd been tanning that morning. I could tell because you could see the marks her goggles had left.

"Oh, we're not having a rehearsal dinner," I said. Because honestly, what was there to rehearse? We were getting married on the beach. It was going to be simple and uncomplicated, the way we both wanted it.

Taylor handed the plate to me. "Then you have to wear it like a hat."

Lucinda got up and tied the paper plate around my head like a bonnet. We all laughed as Marcy took my picture.

Taylor stood up, holding her notebook. "Okay, so get ready for what Belly's going to say on her wedding night."

I covered my face with my ribbon hat. I'd heard of this game before. The maid of honor writes down all the stuff the bride-to-be says while she's opening presents.

"'Oh, so pretty!'" Taylor exclaimed, and the room tittered.

I tried to grab the notebook from her, but she held it above my head and read, "'Jeremiah's gonna love this!'"

After the toilet-paper wedding dress competition, after we helped clean up and everyone had left, I walked my mother to her car.

I felt shy as I said, "Thank you for coming, Mom. It means a lot to me."

She brushed my hair out of my eyes. "You're my girl," she said simply.

I threw my arms around her. "I love you so, so much."

I called Jeremiah as soon as I got in my car. "We are so on!" I screamed. Not that we ever weren't. Still, planning this wedding, being away from home, being in a fight with my mom—it'd had me in knots. But with my mother by my side, I finally felt like I could breathe again. My worries were gone. I finally felt complete. I felt like I could do this.

That night, I slept at home. Steven and my mom and I watched crime TV, one of those shows where they re-create crimes. We howled like wolves at the horrible acting, and we ate Fritos and the rest of my mother's lemon squares. It was so good.

chapter *forty-one*
CONRAD

The day Belly went home, I went to visit Ernie, the old owner of the seafood restaurant I used to bus tables at. Every kid who ever went to Cousins knew who Ernie was, just like Ernie knew every kid. He never forgot a face, no matter how old he got. Ernie had to have been at least seventy years old when I worked there in high school. His nephew John was running the place now, and he was a prick. At first he demoted Ernie to bartending, but Ernie couldn't keep up, so John had him roll silverware. John ended up cutting him out of the business completely, forcing him into retirement. Sure, Ernie was old, but he was a hard worker, and everybody loved him. I used to take smoke breaks with him outside. I knew it was wrong to let him bum a cigarette, but he was an old guy, and who can really say no to an old guy?

Ernie lived in a small house off the highway, and I tried to go out and see him once a week at least. To keep him company but also to make sure he was still alive. Ernie didn't have anybody around to remind him to take his medicine, and his nephew John sure as hell wasn't coming by to visit. After John pushed him out of the business, Ernie said John wasn't his blood anymore.

So I was pretty surprised when I pulled onto Ernie's street and saw John's car on its way out. I parked in front of the house and knocked once before I let myself in.

"Did you bring me a cigarette?" Ernie asked me from the couch.

It was the same thing every time. He wasn't even allowed to smoke anymore. "No," I said. "I quit."

"Then get the hell out."

Then he laughed the way he always did, and I sat on his couch. We watched old cop shows and ate peanuts in silence. During commercial breaks, that was when we'd talk.

"Did you hear my brother's getting married next weekend?" I asked.

He snorted. "I'm not in the ground yet, boy. 'Course I heard. Everybody's heard. She's a sweet girl. Used to curtsy at me when she was little."

Grinning, I said, "That's because we told her you used to be a prince in Italy but then you became a mafioso. The Godfather of Cousins."

"Damn straight."

The show came back on, and we watched in comfortable silence. Then, at the next break, Ernie said, "So are you gonna cry about it like a punk, or are you gonna do something?"

I almost choked on my peanut. Coughing, I said, "What are you talking about?"

He made another snorty sound. "Don't be cute with me. You love her, right? She's the one?"

"Ernie, I think you forgot to take your meds today," I said. "Where's your pillbox?"

He waved me off with one bony white hand, his attention back on the TV. "Simmer down. Show's back on."

I had to wait until the next commercial until I asked him casually, "Do you really believe in that? That people are meant to be with one person?"

Shelling a nut, he said, "Sure I do. Elizabeth was my one. When she passed, I didn't figure a reason to look for another one. My girl was gone. Now I'm just biding my time. Get me a beer, will you?"

I stood up and went to his fridge. I came back with a beer and a fresh glass. Ernie had a thing about a fresh glass. "What was John doing over here?" I asked. "I saw him on my way in."

"He came to mow my lawn."

"I thought that was my job," I said, pouring the beer into his glass.

"You do a shit job of edging."

"When did you guys even start speaking again?"

Ernie shrugged and popped a peanut into his mouth. "He's probably just sniffing around here so I leave him my property when I kick it." He drank his beer and leaned back into his easy chair. "Eh, he's a good kid. My sister's only son. He's family. Family's family. Never forget that, Conrad."

"Ernie, two commercial breaks ago, you told me that if I didn't try and break up my brother's wedding, I was a punk!"

Picking at his teeth, Ernie said, "If a girl's the one, all bets are off, family or no family."

I felt lighter when I left Ernie's house a couple of hours later. I always did.

chapter *forty-two*

It was Wednesday, just a few days before the wedding. Tomorrow, Taylor and Anika were coming up to Cousins, and so were Josh, Redbird, and my brother. The boys were going to have their so-called bachelor night, and Taylor and Anika and I were just going to hang by the pool. Between Denise Coletti and Taylor, the wedding was pretty much ready to go. The food had been ordered— lobster rolls and shrimp cocktail. We had Christmas lights for the deck and yard. Conrad was going to play a song on the guitar when I walked out with my dad. I was going to wear the jewelry Susannah had left me; I was going to do my own hair and makeup.

Everything was coming together, but I still couldn't shake the feeling that there was something I'd forgotten.

I was vacuuming the living room when Conrad

pushed open the sliding door. He'd been surfing all morning. I turned off the vacuum cleaner. "What's wrong?" I asked him. He looked pale, and his hair was dripping in his eyes.

"Wipeout," he said. "I got cut by my fin."

"Bad?"

"Nah, not too bad." I watched him limp over to the bathroom, and I ran over. He was sitting on the sill of the tub, and blood was soaking through his towel and running down his leg. I felt woozy for a split second.

"It's already stopped bleeding," Conrad said, and his face was as white as the marble counter. He looked like he was going to pass out. "Looks worse than it is."

"Keep putting pressure on it," I said. "I'm gonna get some stuff to clean it."

It must have really hurt, because he obeyed me. When I came back with hydrogen peroxide and gauze and Bactine, he was still sitting there in the same position, his leg in the tub.

I sat down next to him and straddled the sill, facing him. "Let go," I told him.

"I'm fine," he said. "I'll do it."

"No, you're not fine," I said.

Then he let go of the towel, and I pressed down on it. He winced.

"Sorry," I said. I held it for a few minutes, and then I peeled the bloody towel away from his leg. The cut was a few inches long and skinny. It wasn't bleeding as heavily, so I went ahead and started to pour hydrogen peroxide on the wound.

"Ow!" he yelped.

"Don't be such a baby, it's barely a scratch," I lied. I was wondering if he was going to need stitches.

Conrad leaned in closer to me, his head just barely resting on my shoulder as I cleaned. I could feel him breathing in and out, could feel each sharp intake of breath every time I touched the cut.

When the cut was clean, it looked a lot better. I dabbed Bactine on it and then wrapped his calf in gauze. Then I patted his knee. "See? All better."

He lifted his head up and said, "Thank you."

"Sure," I said.

There was this moment between us then, of us just looking at each other, holding each other's gaze. My breath quickened. If I leaned forward just a little, we would be kissing. I knew I should move away, but I couldn't.

"Belly?" I could feel his breath on my neck.

"Yeah?"

"Will you help me stand up? I'm going to go upstairs and take a nap."

"You've lost a lot of blood," I said, and my voice vibrated off the bathroom tiles. "I don't think you're supposed to sleep."

He smiled weakly. "That's with concussions."

I scrambled up and then pulled him up next to me. "Can you walk?" I asked.

"I'll manage," he said, limping away from me, his hand on the wall.

My T-shirt was damp from his head on my shoulder. Mechanically, I started cleaning up the mess, and my heart was pounding out of my chest. What just happened? What did I almost do? This time wasn't like with the peaches. This time it was all me.

Conrad slept right through dinnertime, and I wondered if I should bring him some food but decided against it. Instead I heated up one of the frozen pizzas I'd bought, and then I spent the rest of the night cleaning the downstairs. I was relieved that everybody would be here tomorrow. It wouldn't be just me and him anymore. Once Jeremiah was here, everything would go back to normal.

chapter *forty-three*

Everything did go back to normal. I was normal, Conrad was normal: it was like nothing happened. Because nothing did happen. If he didn't have a bandage on his leg, I'd have thought I dreamed the whole thing.

The boys were all down by the beach, except for Conrad, who couldn't get water on his leg. He was in the kitchen, getting meat ready for the grill. Us girls were lying by the pool, passing a bag of kettle corn back and forth. Weatherwise, it was a perfect Cousins day. The sun was high and hot, and there were only a few clouds. No rain in the forecast for the next seven days. Our wedding was safe.

"Redbird's kind of cute, no?" Taylor said, adjusting her bikini top.

"Gross," Anika said. "Anybody with a nickname like Redbird—no thank you."

Taylor frowned at her. "Don't be so judgmental. Belly, what do you think?"

"Um . . . he's a nice guy. Jeremiah says he's very loyal."

"See?" Taylor crowed, poking Anika with her toe.

Anika gave me a look, and I smiled a sneaky smile and said, "He's very, very loyal. So what if he's, like, a smidge Cro-Magnon?"

Taylor threw a handful of popcorn at me and, giggling, I tried to catch some with my mouth.

"Are we going out with the boys tonight?" Anika asked.

"No, they're doing their own thing. They're going to some bar with half-off Irish car bombs or something."

"Eww," Taylor said.

Glancing back toward the kitchen, Anika said in a low voice, "You guys never told me how hot Conrad is."

"He's not *that* hot," Taylor said. "He just thinks he is."

"No he doesn't," I defended. To Anika, I said, "Tay's just mad because he never went for her."

"Why would he go for her when he was your man?"

I shushed her. "He was never my man," I whispered.

"He was *always* your man," Taylor said, spritzing herself with more suntan oil.

Firmly, I said, "Not anymore."

For dinner we had steaks and grilled vegetables. It was a grown-up kind of meal. Drinking red wine, sitting around a table with all my friends, I felt adult. I was sitting next to Jeremiah, and he had his arm around my chair. And yet.

All night, I talked to other people. I didn't look in his direction, but I always knew where he was. I was painfully aware of him. When he was nearby, my body hummed. When he was away, there was this dull ache. With him near, I felt everything.

He was sitting next to Anika, and he said something that made her laugh. I could feel my heart pinch. I looked away.

Tom stood up and made a toast. "To Belly and J-Fish, a really"—he belched—"amazing couple. Really freaking amazing."

I saw Anika give Taylor a look, like *you think this guy is cute?* Taylor shrugged back at her. Everyone lifted their beer cans and wine glasses, and we clinked. Jeremiah pulled me to him and kissed me on the lips, in front of everyone. I pulled away, feeling embarrassed. I saw the look on Conrad's face and wished I hadn't.

Then Steven said, "One more toast, guys." Awkwardly, he stood up. "I've known Jere my whole life. Belly too, unfortunately."

I threw my napkin at him.

"You guys are good together," Steven said, looking at me. Then he looked at Jeremiah. "Treat her right, man. She's a pain in the ass, but she's the only sister I've got."

I could feel myself tear up. I got up and hugged him. "You jerk," I said, wiping my eyes.

As I sat back down next to Jere, he said, "I guess I should say something too. First, thanks for coming, you guys. Josh, Redbird. Taylor and Anika. It means a lot to have you here with us." Jere nudged me, and I stared up at him, waiting for him to mention Conrad. I gave him a pointed look, but he didn't seem to get it. He said, "You say something too, Belly."

"Thanks for coming," I echoed. "And, Conrad, thanks for this amazing meal. Really freaking amazing."

Everyone laughed.

After dinner, I went up to Jeremiah's room and watched him get ready to go out with the boys. The girls were staying behind. I'd told Taylor she could go and get her flirt on with Redbird, but she said she'd rather stay. "He ate his steak with his hands," she'd said, looking sick.

Jere was putting on deodorant, and I was sitting on his unmade bed. "You sure you don't want to come with us?" he asked.

"I'm sure." Suddenly, I said, "Hey, remember that time when you found that dog on the beach? And we named her Rosie until we realized she was a boy, and then we still kept calling her Rosie anyway?"

He looked at me, frowning slightly, remembering. "It wasn't me who found her, it was Conrad."

"No, it wasn't. It was you. And you cried when her owners came and got her."

"No, that was Conrad." His voice was hard all of a sudden.

"I don't think so," I said.

"It definitely was."

"Are you sure?" I asked him.

"I'm positive. Steve and I gave him so much shit for crying."

Had it really been Conrad? I'd been so sure of that memory.

We had Rosie for three glorious days before someone claimed her. Rosie was sweet. She was yellow and she had soft fur and we fought over whose bed she would sleep in at night. We decided to take turns, and my turn was last because I was the youngest, so I never got to keep her in my bed.

What else had I remembered wrong? I was a person who loved to play Remember When in my head. I'd always prided myself on how I remembered every detail. It scared me to think that my memories could be just ever-so-slightly wrong.

chapter *forty-four*

After the boys left, we went up to my room to do nails and practice makeup for the wedding. "I still think you should get your makeup done," Taylor said from my bed. She was doing her toes a pale, chalky pink.

"I don't want to spend any more of Mr. Fisher's money. He's spending enough as it is," I said. "Besides, I hate wearing a lot of makeup. I never look like me."

"They're professionals—they know what they're doing."

"That time you took me to the MAC counter, they made me look like a drag queen," I said.

"That's their aesthetic," Taylor said. "At least let me put false eyelashes on you. I'm wearing them. So is Anika."

I looked at Anika, who was lying on the floor with a cucumber face mask on. "Your eyelashes are already long," I said.

"She's making me," Anika said through gritted teeth, trying not to crack her mask.

"Well, I'm not wearing them," I said. "Jere knows what my real eyelashes look like, and he doesn't care. Besides, they make my eyes itch. Remember, Tay? You put them on me for Halloween, and I took them off as soon as you had your back turned."

"A waste of fifteen dollars," Taylor sniffed. She slid off the bed and sat next to me on the floor. I was trying on the different lipsticks Taylor had brought with her. So far it was between a rosy pink lip gloss and an apricot lipstick.

"Which do you like better?" I asked her. I had the gloss on my top lip and the lipstick on my bottom lip.

"The lipstick," Taylor said. "It'll pop better in pictures."

At first we were just going to have Josh take pictures— he'd taken a couple of photography classes at Finch, and he was the official frat photographer for all their parties. But now that Mr. Fisher and Denise Coletti were involved, we'd hired an actual photographer, someone Denise knew.

"I might still get my hair done," Taylor said.

"Go for it," I told her.

We all changed into our pajamas, and Taylor and Anika presented me with a wedding gift—a lacy white babydoll nightie with matching panties.

"For the wedding night," Taylor said meaningfully.

"Uh, yeah, I got that," I said, holding up the underwear. I hoped I wasn't blushing too red. "Thanks, guys."

"Do you have any questions for us?" Taylor asked, perching on my bed.

"Taylor! I, like, live in the world. I'm not an idiot."

"I'm just saying . . ." She paused. "You probably won't like it that much the first couple of times. I mean, I'm super tiny, which means I'm really little down there, so it hurt a lot. It might not hurt as bad for you. Tell her, Anika."

Anika rolled her eyes. "It didn't hurt me at all, Iz."

"Well, you probably have a large vagina," Taylor said.

Anika thumped Taylor on the head with a pillow, and we all started giggling and couldn't stop. Then I said, "Wait, exactly how bad did it hurt, Tay? Did it hurt the way a punch in the stomach hurts?"

"Who's ever punched you in the stomach?" Anika asked me.

"I have an older brother," I reminded her.

"It's a different kind of pain," Taylor said.

"Did it hurt worse than period cramps?"

"Yes. But I would say it's more comparable to getting a shot of Novocain in your gums."

"Great, now she's comparing losing your virginity to getting a cavity filled," Anika said, getting up. "Iz, quit listening to her. I promise you it's more fun than going to the dentist. It would be one thing if you were both virgins, but Jeremiah knows what's up. He'll take care of you."

Taylor collapsed into another fit of giggles. "He'll take *care* of her!"

I tried to smile, but my face felt frozen. Jeremiah had been with two other girls. His high school girlfriend, Mara, and now Lacie Barone. So yeah, I was pretty sure he'd know what to do. I just wished he didn't.

We were all lying in my bed, side by side by side. We were just talking with the lights off, and Anika fell asleep first. I'd been going over and over it, whether or not I should confide in Taylor, tell her about Conrad, how mixed up I'd been feeling. I wanted to tell her, but I was also afraid.

"Tay?" I whispered. She was lying next to me, and I was on the edge of the bed because I was going to leave and sleep in Jere's room when the boys came back.

"What?" Her voice was sleepy.

"Something weird happened."

"What?" She was alert now.

"Yesterday, Conrad cut his leg up surfing, and I helped him, and there was this weird moment between us."

"Did you kiss?" she hissed.

"No!" But then I whispered, "But I wanted to. I was—I was tempted to."

"Whoa," she said with a little sigh. "But nothing *happened*, right?"

"Nothing happened. I just feel . . . freaked out because I kind of wanted it to. Just for a second." I let out a big breath. "I'm getting married in a couple of days. I shouldn't be thinking about kissing other boys."

Softly, she said, "Conrad's not other boys. He's your first love. Your first great love."

"You're right!" I said, relieved. I felt lighter already. "It's nostalgia. That's all this is."

Taylor hesitated and then said, "There's something I haven't told you. Conrad went to see your mom."

My breath caught. "When?"

"A couple of weeks ago. He convinced her to come to the bridal shower. She told my mom, and my mom told me. . . ."

I was silent. He did that for me?

"I didn't tell you, because I didn't want it to get you all mixed up again. Because you love Jere, right? You want to marry him?"

"Uh-huh."

"Are you sure? Because it's not too late, you know. You could still call the whole thing off—you don't have to do this this weekend. You could take some more time. . . ."

"I don't need more time," I said.

"Okay."

I rolled over. "Good night, Tay."

"Good night."

It took a while before her breathing turned heavy and regular, and I just lay there next to her, thinking.

Conrad was still looking out for me. Silently, I got out of bed, crossed the room, and felt my way around my bureau until I found it. My glass unicorn.

chapter *forty-five*

When Susannah would drop us off at the mall or the Putt Putt, she would put Conrad in charge every time. She'd say, "Take care of them, Connie. I'm counting on you."

There was this time we split up at the mall, because the boys wanted to go to the arcade and I didn't. I was eight. I said I'd meet them in the food court in one hour. I went straight to the glass-blower shop. The boys never wanted to go in the glass-blower shop, but I loved it. I'd wander from counter to counter. I especially liked looking at the glass unicorns. I wanted to buy one, just a little one, but they were twelve dollars. I only had ten. I couldn't stop looking at the unicorn. I'd pick it up then put it down again then pick it up again. Before I knew it, more than an hour had passed, almost two. I ran back to the food court as fast as I could. I worried the boys had left without me.

When I showed up, Conrad wasn't there. Jeremiah and Steven were sitting in the Taco Bell section counting their arcade tickets. "Where have you been?" Steven said, looking annoyed.

I ignored him. "Where's Conrad?" I asked Jeremiah, panting.

"He went off looking for you," Jeremiah said. To Steven, he said, "Do you want to use our tickets to buy something now or save up a ton for next time?"

"Let's wait," Steven said. "The guy told me they're getting more prizes next week."

When Conrad came back a little while later to find me sitting with Jeremiah and Steven and eating an ice cream cone, he looked so mad. "Where were you?" he yelled. "You were supposed to be back here at three!"

I could feel a lump in my throat, and I knew I was about to cry. "At the glass-blower shop," I whispered, my Moose Tracks ice cream dripping in my hand.

"If something happened to you, my mom would have killed me! I'm the one she left in charge."

"There was this unicorn . . ."

"Forget it. You're not coming anywhere with us anymore."

"No, Conrad! Come on," I cried, brushing my tears away with my sticky hand. "I'm sorry."

He felt bad for yelling, I could tell. He sat down next to me and said, "Don't ever do that again, Belly. From now on, we stick together. Okay?"

"Okay," I said, sniffling.

For my birthday that August, Conrad gave me a glass unicorn. Not the small one, but the big one that cost twenty dollars. Its horn broke off during one of Jeremiah and Steven's wrestling matches, but I kept it. I kept it right on top of my bureau. How could I have thrown such a gift away?

chapter *forty-six*
CONRAD

I volunteered to be the DD. By the time we left the house, everyone was already pretty sloppy from the wine and beer.

We took that kid Tom or Redbird or whatever-his-name-is's car because it was the biggest. It was practically a Hummer. Jere sat in the passenger seat next to me, and the other guys sat in the back.

Tom reached up between us and turned the radio on. He started to rap with the music, off beat and wrong lyrics. Josh joined him, and Steven opened up the sunroof and stuck his head out.

With a sidelong glance at Jere, I said, "These are your friends?"

He laughed and started rapping too.

The bar was packed. Girls everywhere in high heels

and glossy lipstick, with their hair shiny and straight. Right away, Redbird started trying to dance on every girl that walked by. Shot down each and every time.

I went to the bar to get the first round, and Steven followed me. We were waiting to get the bartender's attention when he clapped his hand on my shoulder and said, "So how are you doing with this whole thing?"

"What? The wedding?"

"Yeah."

I turned away from him. "It is what it is."

"Do you think it's a mistake?"

I didn't have to answer him, because the bartender finally looked our way. "Five double shots of tequila and a Newcastle," I said.

Steven said, "You're not going to take a shot with us?"

"I've got to take care of you numskulls, remember?"

We carried the shots back to the table where the other guys were sitting. All five guys pounded them back, and then Redbird got up and started beating his chest and yelling like Tarzan. The guys busted up laughing and started egging him on to go talk to a couple of girls on the dance floor. He and Steven went over to them, and we all sat back and watched. Steven was having better luck than Redbird. He and the red-haired girl started dancing, and Redbird came back to our table, dejected.

"I'll get us another round," I said. I figured it was my duty as best man to get them all wasted.

I came back with five more shots of tequila, and since Steven was still out on the dance floor, Jere downed his shot.

I was nursing my beer when I heard that guy Josh say to Jeremiah, "Dude, you're finally gonna get to close with Belly."

My head snapped up. Jeremiah had his arm slung around Josh while he sang, "It's a nice day for a white wedding."

They hadn't had sex yet?

Then I heard Josh say, "Yo, you're, like, a virgin now too. You haven't gotten any since Lacie in Cabo."

Cabo? Jeremiah had gone to Cabo this past spring break. When he and Belly were a couple.

Jeremiah started to sing, off-key, "Like a virgin, touched for the very first time." Then he stood up. "I gotta piss."

I watched him stumble off to the bathroom, and Josh said, "Fisher's a lucky bastard. Lacie is smokin'."

Tom elbowed him and said, loudly, "Shit, remember how they locked us out of the hotel room?" To me, he said, "This is hilarious, man. Hilarious. They locked us out, and they were so into it, they didn't even hear us knocking. We had to sleep in the friggin' hallway that night."

Laughing, Josh said, "That girl was hella loud, too. Oh, Jere-uhhh-mi-uhhh…"

I saw red. Under the tables, I clenched my fists. I wanted to hit something. First I wanted to hit these two guys, and then I wanted to go find my brother and beat the shit out of him.

I jumped up from the table and made my way across the club, shouldering and pushing my way through the crowd until I got to the bathroom.

I banged on the door.

"Somebody's in here," Jeremiah slurred from inside. Then I heard him retch into the toilet.

I stood there another few seconds, and then I walked away, past our table and out to the parking lot.

chapter *forty-seven*

An hour later, the boys came back, drunk as skunks.
I'd seen Jere drunk before, but not like this. He was so
wasted, the boys practically had to carry him upstairs. He
could barely open his eyes. "Belllllly," he called out. "I'm
gonna marry you, girl."

From the bottom of the staircase, I yelled back, "Go
to sleep!"

Conrad wasn't with them. I asked Tom, "Where's
Conrad? I thought he was your designated driver."

Tom was swaying upstairs. "I dunno. He was with us."

I went out to the car, thinking maybe he'd passed out
in the backseat. But he wasn't there. I was starting to get
worried, but just then I caught a glimpse of him way
down the beach, sitting in the lifeguard stand. I took off
my shoes and made my way over to him.

"Come down," I called up. "Don't fall asleep up there."

"Come up," he said. "Just for a minute."

I thought about it for a second. He didn't sound drunk; he sounded fine. I climbed up the side of the chair and sat next to him. "Did you guys have fun?" I asked him.

He didn't answer me.

I watched the water lap along the shore. There was a crescent moon. I said, "I love it here at night."

And then, suddenly, he said, "I have to tell you something."

Something in his voice scared me. "What?"

Looking out at the ocean, he said, "Jere cheated on you when he was in Cabo."

That wasn't what I expected him to say. It was maybe the last thing I expected him to say. His jaw was clenched, and he looked angry. "Tonight at the club, one of his dumbass friends said something." He finally looked at me. "I'm sorry you had to hear it from me. I thought you had a right to know."

I didn't know how to answer him. I finally said, "I already knew about it."

His head jerked back. "You knew?"

"Yeah."

"And you're still marrying him?"

My cheeks felt hot. "He made a mistake," I said softly. "He hates himself for what he did. I forgave him. Everything's fine now. Everything's really great."

Conrad's mouth curled in disgust. "Are you kidding me? He spent the night in a hotel room with some girl and you're defending him?"

"Who are you to judge us? It's none of your business."

"None of my business? That shithead is my brother, and you're . . ." He didn't finish his sentence. Instead he said, "I never thought you'd be the kind of girl who would put up with that from a guy."

"I put up with a lot worse from you." I said it automatically. I said it without thinking.

Eyes flashing, he said, "I never once cheated on you. I never even looked at another girl when we were together."

I slid away from him and started to climb down. "I don't want to talk about this anymore." I didn't know why he was bringing any of this up now. I just wanted it all to go away.

"I thought I knew you," he said.

"I guess you thought wrong," I said. Then I jumped the rest of the way down.

I heard him jump down behind me, and I started to walk away. I could feel tears coming, and I didn't want him to see.

Conrad ran up behind me and grabbed my arm. I tried to turn my head away from him, but he saw, and his face changed. He felt sorry for me. That only made me feel worse. "I'm sorry," he said. "I shouldn't have said anything. You're right. It's not my business."

I spun away from him. I didn't need his pity.

I started walking in the opposite direction of the house. I didn't know where I was going, I just wanted to get away from him.

He called out, "I still love you."

I froze. And then slowly, I turned around to look at him. "Don't say that."

He took a step closer. "I don't know if I'll ever get you out of my system, not completely. I have . . . this feeling. That you'll always be there. Here." Conrad clawed at his heart and then dropped his hand.

"It's only because I'm marrying Jeremiah." I hated the way my voice sounded—shaky and small. Weak. "That's why you're saying all this all of a sudden."

"It's not all of a sudden," he said, his eyes locked on mine. "It's always."

"It doesn't matter. It's too late." I turned away from him.

"Wait," he said. He grabbed my arm again.

"Let go of me," I said, and my voice was so cold, I wouldn't have recognized it. It surprised him, too.

He flinched, and his hand dropped. "Just tell me one thing. Why get married now?" he said. "Why not just live together?"

I had asked myself the same question. I still hadn't come up with a good answer.

I started to walk away, but he followed me. He wrapped his arms around me, over my shoulders.

"Let go." I struggled, but he held on.

"Wait. Wait."

My heart was racing. What if someone saw us? What if someone heard? "If you don't let go of me, I'm going to scream."

"Hear me out, just for a minute. Please. I'm begging you." He sounded strangled and hoarse.

I let out a breath. In my head I started to count backward. Sixty seconds was all he would get from me. I would let him talk for sixty seconds, and then I would go and not look back. Two years ago, this was all I wanted to hear from him. But it was too late now.

Quietly, he said, "Two years ago, I fucked up. But not in the way you think. That night—do you remember that night? The night we were driving back from school and it was raining so hard, we had to stop at that motel. Do you remember?"

I remembered that night. Of course I did.

"That night, I didn't sleep at all. I stayed up, thinking about what to do. What was the right thing to do? Because I knew I loved you. But I knew I shouldn't. I didn't have the right to love anybody then. After my mom died, I was so pissed off. I had this anger in me all the time. I felt like I was going to erupt any minute."

He drew his breath in. "I didn't have it in me to love you the way you deserved. But I knew who did. Jere. He loved you. If I kept you with me, I was going to hurt you somehow. I knew it. I couldn't have it. So I let you go."

I'd stopped counting by then. I just concentrated on breathing. In and out.

"But this summer . . . God, this summer. Being near you again, talking the way we used to talk. You looking at me the way you used to."

I closed my eyes. It didn't matter what he said now. That was what I told myself.

"I see you again, and everything I planned goes to shit. It's impossible. . . . I love Jere more than anybody. He's my brother, my family. I hate myself for doing this. But when I see you two together, I hate him too." His voice broke. "Don't marry him. Don't be with him. Be with me."

His shoulders shook. He was crying. Hearing him beg like this, seeing him exposed and vulnerable, it felt like my heart was breaking. There were so many things I wanted to say to him. But I couldn't. With Conrad, once I started, I couldn't stop.

I broke away from him roughly. "Conrad—"

He grabbed me. "Just tell me. Do you still feel anything for me?"

I pushed him away. "No! Don't you get it? You will never be what Jere is to me. He's my best friend. He loves me no matter what. He doesn't take it away whenever he feels like it. Nobody has ever treated me the way he does. Nobody. Least of all you.

"You and I," I said, and then I stopped. I had to get this

right. I had to make it so that he let me go forever. "You and I were never anything."

His face went slack. I saw the light die out in his eyes. I couldn't look at him anymore.

I started walking again, and this time he didn't follow me. I didn't look back. Couldn't look back. If I saw his face again, I might not be able to leave.

As I walked, I told myself, Hold it, hold it, just a little longer. Only when I was sure he couldn't see me, only when the house was in sight again, that was when I let myself cry. I dropped down in the sand and cried for Conrad and then for me. I cried for what was never going to be.

It's a known fact that in life, you can't have everything. In my heart I knew I loved them both, as much as it is possible to love two people at the same time. Conrad and I were linked, we would always be linked. That wasn't something I could do away with. I knew that now—that love wasn't something you could erase, no matter how hard you tried.

I got up, I brushed the sand from my body, and I went inside the house. I climbed into Jeremiah's bed, next to him. He was passed out, snoring loudly the way he did when he drank too much.

"I love you," I said to his back.

chapter *forty-eight*

Late the next morning, Taylor and Anika went into town to pick up some last-minute things. I stayed behind to clean the bathrooms, since the parents were arriving later that day. The boys were all still asleep, which was a good thing. I didn't know what I would or wouldn't say to Jeremiah. The worry was eating me up inside. Would it be selfish or would it be merciful not to say anything?

I ran into Conrad on my way out of the shower, and I couldn't even look him in the eye. I heard his car leave soon after. I didn't know where he'd gone, but I hoped he'd stay far away from me. It felt too raw, too soon. I found myself wishing that either he or I wasn't there. I couldn't leave—I was the one getting married—but I wished he would. It would make things easier. It was a selfish thought, I knew. It was half Conrad's house, after all.

After I'd made the beds and straightened up the guest bathroom, I went down to the kitchen to make myself a sandwich. I thought I was safe, I thought he was still out. But there he was, eating a sandwich himself.

As soon as he saw me, Conrad put down his sandwich. Roast beef, it looked like. "Can I talk to you for a sec?"

"I'm about to go into town to run some errands," I said, looking somewhere in the vicinity of over his shoulder, anywhere but at him. "Wedding stuff."

I started to walk away, but he followed me out to the porch.

"Listen, I'm sorry about last night."

I didn't say anything.

"Will you do me a favor? Will you just forget everything I said?" He flashed a slight, ironic kind of smile. I wanted to smack the smile off his face. "I was out of my mind last night, drunk off my ass. Being here again, it just brought back a lot of stuff. But it's all ancient history, I know that. Honestly, I can barely remember what I said, but I'm sure that whatever it was, it was out of line. I'm really sorry."

For a moment I felt such rage, I think I forgot how to speak. I found it was hard to catch my breath. I felt like a flopping goldfish, opening and closing my mouth, sucking in pockets of air. I hadn't even slept the night before; instead, I'd agonized over every word he said to me. I felt so stupid. And to think, just for a second, just for a moment, I had wavered. I had pictured it, what it would be like, if I was marrying *him* and not Jeremiah. I hated him for that.

"You weren't drunk," I said.

"Yeah, I really was." This time he gave me an apologetic smile.

I ignored it. "You brought up all that the weekend of my wedding, and now you want me to just 'forget it'? You're sick. Don't you get that you can't play with people like that?"

Conrad's smile faded. "Hold on a second. Belly—"

"Don't say my name." I backed away from him. "Don't even think it. In fact, don't ever speak to me again."

Again with the ironic half smile, he said, "Well, that would be kind of hard, considering the fact that you're marrying my brother. Come on, Belly."

I didn't think I could be angrier, and now I was. I was so mad, I practically spat as I said, "I want you to leave. Make up one of your bullshit excuses and just go. Go back to Boston or California. I don't care where. I just want you gone."

His eye twitched. "I'm not leaving."

"Go," I said, shoving him, hard. "Just go."

That's when I saw the first cracks in his armor.

His voice cracking, he said, "What did you expect me to say to you, Belly?"

"Stop saying my name!" I screamed.

"What do you want from me?" he yelled back. "I laid myself fucking bare last night! I put it all out there, and you shut me down. Rightfully so. I get that I shouldn't have said any of that stuff to you. But now here I am trying to find a way to come out of this with just a little fragment of pride so I can look you in the eye when this is all over, and you won't even let me have that. You broke my heart last night, all right? Is that what you want to hear?"

Again, I was at a loss for words. And then I found them. I said, "You really are heartless."

"No, I think you might actually be the heartless one," he said.

He was already walking away as I called out, "What is that supposed to mean?" I walked up right behind and twisted his arm toward me so we were facing each other. "Tell me what you meant by that."

"You know what it means." Conrad jerked away from me. "I still love you. I never stopped. I think you know it. I think you've known it all along."

I pressed my lips together, shaking my head. "That's not true."

"Don't lie."

I shook my head again.

"Have it your way. But I'm not going to pretend for you anymore." With that, he walked down the steps and to his car.

I sank onto the deck. My heart was pounding a million trillion times a minute. I never felt more alive. Anger, sadness, joy. He made me feel it all. No one else had that kind of effect on me. No one.

Suddenly I had this feeling, this absolute certainty, that I was never going to be able to let him go. It was as simple and as hard as that. I had clung to him like a barnacle all these years, and now I couldn't cut away. It was my own fault, really. I couldn't let go of Conrad, and I couldn't walk away from Jeremiah.

Where did that leave me?

I was getting married tomorrow.

If I did it, if I chose Conrad, I could never go back. I would never cup the back of Jere's neck in my hand again, feel its downy softness. Like feathers. Jere would never look at me the way he did now. He looked at me like I was his girl. Which I was, and it felt like it had always been that way. That would all be lost. Over. Some things you can't take back. How was I supposed to say good-bye to all of those things? I couldn't. And what about our families? What would it do to my mother, his father? It would destroy us. I couldn't do that. Especially—especially with everything so fragile now that Susannah was gone. We were still figuring out how to all be together without her, how to still be that summer family.

I couldn't give all that up, just for this. Just for Conrad.

Conrad, who told me he loved me. At last, he said the words.

When Conrad Fisher told a girl he loved her, he meant it. A girl could believe in that. A girl could maybe even bet her whole life on it.

That was what I would be doing. I would be betting my whole life on him. And I couldn't do it. I wouldn't.

chapter *forty-nine*
CONRAD

I was in my car, driving away, my adrenaline pumping hard.

I finally said it. The actual words, out loud, to her face. It was a relief, not carrying it around anymore, and it was a rush, actually telling her. I was in an elated sort of daze, on a high. She loved me. I didn't need to hear her say it out loud, I knew it innately in the way she looked at me just then.

But now what? If she loved me and I loved her, what did we do now, when there were so many people in between us? How could I ever get to her? Did I have it in me to just grab her hand and run away? I believed she'd come with me. If I asked her, I believed she really might come. But where would we even go? Would they forgive us? Jere, Laurel, my dad. And if I really did take her away, where would I be leading her?

Beyond that, the questions and the doubts, in the pit of my stomach, there was all this regret. If I had told her a year ago, a month ago, even a week ago, would things be different now? It was the day before her wedding. In twenty-four hours, she would be married to my brother. Why did I wait so long?

I drove around for a while, into town and then along the water, then I went back to the house. None of the cars were parked in the driveway, so I thought I was home free for a while—but then there was Taylor sitting on the front porch.

"Where is everybody?" I asked her.

"Well hello to you, too." She pushed her sunglasses to the top of her head. "They went sailing."

"Why didn't you go with them?"

"I get seasick." Taylor eyed me. "I need to talk to you."

Warily, I eyed her back. "About what?"

She pointed at the chair next to hers. "Come sit down first."

I sat.

"What did you say to Belly last night?"

Averting my eyes, I said, "What did she tell you?"

"Nothing. But I can tell something's wrong. I know she was crying last night. Her eyes were completely swollen this morning. I would be willing to bet money that she was crying because of you. Again. Nice one, Conrad."

I could feel my chest tighten. "It's none of your business."

Taylor glared at me. "Belly is my oldest friend in the world. Of course it's my business. I'm warning you, Conrad. Leave her alone. You're confusing her. Again."

I started to stand up. "Are we done?"

"No. Sit your ass back down."

I sat down again.

"Do you have any idea how badly you've hurt her, over and over again? You treat her like a toy that you just pick up and play with whenever you feel like it. You're like a little boy. Someone else took what was yours, and you don't like that one bit, so you swoop in and shit all over everything just because you can."

I exhaled. "That's not what I'm trying to do."

She bit her lip. "Belly told me that a part of her will always love you. Are you still trying to tell me you don't care?"

She said that? "I never said I didn't care."

"You're probably the only one who could stop her from going though with this wedding. But you'd better be damn sure you still want her, because if you don't, you're just effing up their lives for no reason." She put her sunglasses back on. "Don't eff up my best friend's life, Conrad. Don't be a selfish bastard like usual. Be the good guy she says you are. Let her go."

Be the good guy she says you are.

I thought I could do it, fight for her till the end, not think about anyone else. Just grab her hand and run. But if I did that, wouldn't I be proving Belly wrong? I wasn't a good guy. I would be a selfish bastard just like Taylor said. But I would have Belly next to me.

chapter *fifty*

That night, we all had dinner at a newish restaurant in town—my parents, Mr. Fisher, all of us kids. I wasn't hungry, but I ordered a lobster roll and I ate every bite of it, because my dad was paying. He insisted. My dad, who wore the same white dress shirt with gray stripes for every "fancy" occasion. He was wearing it that night, sitting next to my mother in her navy shirtdress, and my heart just swelled with love every time I looked at the two of them.

And there was Taylor, pretending to be interested as my dad went on about a lobster's nervous system. Sitting next to Anika, who actually did look interested. Next to Anika was my brother, who was rolling his eyes.

Conrad sat at the far end of the table, with Jere's friends. I made a conscious effort not to look in his direction, to just keep focused on my plate, on Jeremiah next to me. I didn't have to bother, because Conrad wasn't looking at me either. He was talking to the guys, to Steven, to my mother. To everyone but me. This is what you wanted, I reminded myself. You told him to leave you alone. You asked for this.

You can't have it both ways.

"Are you okay?" Jeremiah whispered.

I lifted my head and smiled at him. "Yeah! Of course. I'm just full."

Jeremiah took one of my fries and said, "Save room for dessert."

I nodded. Then he leaned over and kissed me, and I kissed him back. After, I saw his eyes flicker over to the end of the table, so quick I could have imagined it.

chapter *fifty-one*
CONRAD

I felt like I was going out of my mind that night. Sitting there at the table with everyone, cheersing when my dad made a toast, trying not to watch when Jere kissed her in front of all of us.

After dinner was over, Jere and Belly and all their friends went to the boardwalk for ice cream. My dad and Belly's dad went to their hotel. It was just Laur and me back at the house. I was on my way up to my room, but Laurel stopped me and said, "Hey, let's have a beer, Connie. I think we deserve it, don't you?"

We sat at the kitchen table with our beers. She clinked my bottle and said, "To . . . what should we toast to?"

"What else? To the happy couple."

Without looking at me, Laurel said, "How are you doing?"

"Good," I said. "Great."

"Come on. This is your Laura you're talking to. Tell me. How are you feeling?"

"Honestly?" I swigged my beer. "It's pretty much killing me."

Laurel looked back at me, her face tender. "I'm sorry. I know you love her a lot, kid. This must be really hard on you."

I could feel my throat starting to close up. I tried to clear it, unsuccessfully. I could feel it coming up in my chest, behind my eyes. I was going to cry in front of her. It was the way she said it, it was like my mom was right there, knowing without me having to tell her.

Laurel took my hand and clasped it in hers. I tried to pull it away, but she held on tighter. "We'll get through it tomorrow, I promise. It'll be you and me, kid." Squeezing my hand, she said, "God, I miss your mom."

"Me too."

"We really need her right now, don't we?"

I bowed my head and started to cry.

chapter *fifty-two*

I wanted to sleep in Jeremiah's room that night, but when I started to follow him upstairs, Taylor wagged her finger at me. "Uh-uh. It's bad luck."

So I'd gone to my room, and he'd gone to his.

It was too hot. I couldn't sleep. I'd kick the covers off and flip my pillow over to cool off, but it didn't help. I kept looking at the alarm clock. One o'clock, two o'clock.

When I couldn't stand it anymore, I threw off my sheets and put on my bathing suit. I didn't turn on any lights, I just found my way downstairs in the darkness. The moonlight was enough to guide me. Everyone else was asleep.

I made my way outside, down to the pool. I dove in, held my breath for as long as I could. I could already feel my bones start to relax. When I came back up for air, I floated on my back and looked up at the sky. The stars were out. I loved how quiet it was, how still. The only thing I could hear was the ocean lapping against the sand.

Tomorrow I would become Isabel Fisher. It was what I always wanted, my girlhood dream come true a thousand times over. And I'd wrecked it. Or rather, I was about to wreck it. I had to tell the truth. I couldn't marry Jeremiah tomorrow like this, not with a secret that big between us.

I climbed out of the pool, put the towel around me, and went inside the house, up to Jeremiah's room. He was asleep, but I shook him awake. "I need to talk to you," I said. Water from my hair dripped onto his pillow, onto his face.

Groggily, he said, "Isn't it bad luck?"

"I don't care."

Jeremiah sat up, wiping his cheeks. "What's up?"

"Let's talk outside," I said.

We went down to the porch and sat on a lounge chair.

Without preamble, I said, quietly, "Last night Conrad told me he still has feelings for me."

I could feel Jeremiah's body go rigid beside me. I waited for him to speak, and when he didn't, I went on. "Of course I told him I didn't feel the same way. I wanted to tell you sooner, but then I thought it would be a mistake, that I should keep it to myself—"

"I'm going to kill him," he said, and hearing those

words coming out of his mouth shocked me. He stood up.

I tried to pull him back down next to me, but he resisted. I pleaded, "Jere, no. Don't. Please just sit here and talk to me."

"Why are you protecting him?"

"I'm—I'm not. I'm not."

He looked down at me. "Are you marrying me to erase him?"

"No," I said, and it came out more like a gasp. "No."

"The thing is, Bells, I don't believe you," Jeremiah said, and his voice was strangely flat. "I see the way you look at him. I don't think you've ever looked at me like that. Not even once."

I jumped up and grabbed at his hands desperately, but he pulled away. I was breathing hard when I said, "That's not true, Jere. It's not true at all. What I feel for him is all memories. That's it. It has nothing to do with us. All that's in the past. Can't we just forget the past and make our own future? Just the two of us?"

Levelly, he said, "Is it the past? I know you saw him over Christmas. I know you guys were together here."

I opened my mouth, but no words came out.

"Say something. Go ahead, try to deny it."

"Nothing happened between us, Jere. I promise you. I didn't even know he was gonna be here. The only reason I didn't tell you was—" What was it? Why didn't I tell him? Why couldn't I think of a reason? "I didn't want you to be upset over nothing."

"If it was nothing, you would have told me about it. Instead you kept it a secret. After all that stuff you said to me about trust, you kept that to yourself. I felt like shit for what I did with Lacie, and you and I weren't even together when it happened."

I felt sick inside. "How long have you known?"

"Does it matter?" he snapped.

"Yes, to me it does."

Jeremiah started to back away from me. "I've known since it happened. Conrad mentioned he saw you, he thought I already knew. So of course I had to play it off like I did. Do you know how stupid I felt?"

"I can imagine," I whispered. "Why didn't you say something?" We were standing only five or six feet away from each other, but it felt like miles. It was his eyes. They were so distant.

"I was waiting for you to tell me. And you never did."

"I'm sorry. I'm so sorry. I should have told you. I was wrong." It was stupid. My heart was beating so fast. "I love you. We're getting married tomorrow. Me and you, right?"

When he didn't answer me, I asked again. "Aren't we?"

"I've got to get out of here," he said at last. "I need to think."

"Can I come with you?"

This time the answer came swiftly, and it was devastating. "No," he said.

He left, and I didn't try to follow him. I just sank onto the steps. I couldn't feel my legs. I couldn't feel my body. Was this happening? Was this real? It didn't feel real.

chapter *fifty-three*

Somewhere outside, a goldfinch was singing. Or maybe it was a song sparrow. My dad had tried to teach me the different kinds of bird songs, but I couldn't quite remember.

The sky was gray. It wasn't raining yet. But any minute now, it was going to pour. It was like any other morning in Cousins Beach. Except it wasn't, because I was getting married.

I was reasonably sure I was getting married. The only thing was, I had no idea where Jeremiah had gone or if he was even coming back.

I was sitting at the vanity mirror in my pink bathrobe, trying to curl my hair. Taylor was at the beauty salon, and she'd tried to persuade me to get mine done there too, but I'd said no. The only time I ever got my hair done, I hated the way it looked. Like a beauty pageant contestant, stiff and high. I didn't look like me. I thought that today of all days, I should look like me.

There was a knock at the door.

"Come in," I said, trying to fix a curl that had already gone limp.

The door opened. It was my mother. She was already dressed. She was wearing a suit jacket and linen pants and was carrying a lemon yellow envelope. I recognized it right away: Susannah's personal stationery. It was so like her. I wished I was worthy of it. It hurt to think that I had let her down like this. What would she say if she knew?

My mother closed the door behind her. "Do you want me to help?" she asked.

I handed her the curling iron. She set down the letter on my dresser. She stood behind me, sectioning my hair off into thirds. "Did Taylor do your makeup? It looks nice."

"Yeah, she did. Thanks. You look really nice too."

"I'm not ready for this," she said.

I looked at her in the mirror, winding my hair around the barrel, her head down. My mother was beautiful to me in that moment.

She put her hands on my shoulders and looked at me in the mirror. "This isn't what I wanted for you. But I'm here. This is your wedding day. My only daughter."

I reached over my shoulder and took her hand. She

squeezed my hand tight, so tight it hurt. I wanted to confide in her, to confess that things were a mess, that I didn't even know where Jeremiah was or if I would be getting married after all. But it had taken her so long to get here, and if I raised one single doubt now, that would be more than enough for her to put an end to it. She would throw me over her shoulder and carry me away from this whole wedding.

So all that came out was, "Thank you, Mommy."

"You're welcome," she said. She looked over toward my window. "Do you think the weather will hold?"

"I don't know. I hope so."

"Well, if worst comes to worst, we'll move the wedding inside. No big shakes." Then she handed me the letter. "Susannah wanted you to have this on your wedding day."

My mother kissed me on the top of my head and walked out of the room.

I picked up the letter, ran my fingers along my name, written in Susannah's smooth cursive. Then I put it back down on the dresser. Not yet.

There was a knock at the door. "Who is it?" I asked.

"Steven."

"Come in."

The door opened, and Steven came in, closing it behind him. He was wearing the white linen shirt and khaki shorts all the groomsmen were wearing. "Hey," he said, sitting down on my bed. "Your hair looks nice."

"Is he back?"

Steven hesitated.

"Just tell me, Steven."

"No. He's not back. Conrad went off to find him. He thinks he knows where Jere went."

I let out a breath. I was relieved, but at the same time—what would Jeremiah do when he saw Conrad? What if it only made things worse?

"He's going to call as soon as he finds him."

I nodded, then picked up the curling iron again. My fingers trembled, and I had to steady my hand so I wouldn't burn my cheek.

"Did you tell Mom anything?" Steven asked.

"No. I haven't told anybody. So far there's nothing to tell." I wound a piece of hair around the barrel. "He'll be here. I know he will." And I mostly believed it.

"Yeah," Steven said. "Yeah, I'm sure you're right. Do you want me to stay with you?"

I shook my head. "I need to get ready."

"You sure?"

"Yeah. Just let me know as soon as you hear something."

Steven stood up. "I will." Then he came over and patted my shoulder awkwardly. "Everything's going to work out, Belly."

"Yup, I know it will. Don't worry about me. Just find Jere."

As soon as he was gone, I set the curling iron down again. My hand was shaking. I would probably burn myself if I didn't give it a rest. My hair was curled enough anyway.

He was coming back. He was coming back. I knew he was.

And then, because there was nothing left to do, I put on my wedding dress.

I was sitting at the window, watching my dad string Christmas lights on the back porch, when Taylor burst into the room.

Her hair was in an updo, and it looked tight around her forehead. She was carrying a brown paper bag and an ice coffee. "Okay, so, I brought lunch, Anika's helping your mom set the tables up, and this weather isn't doing my hair any favors," Taylor announced, all in one breath. "And I don't know how to tell you this, but I'm pretty sure I felt a raindrop on the way inside." Then she said, "Why are you already in your dress? There's still loads of time before the wedding. Take it off. It's going to get all wrinkly."

When I didn't answer her, she asked, "What's wrong?"

"Jeremiah isn't here," I said.

"Well, of course he isn't here, dummy. It's bad luck to see the bride before the ceremony."

"He's not at home. He left last night, and he hasn't come back." My voice was surprisingly calm. "I told him everything."

Her eyes bulged. "What do you mean, everything?"

"The other day, Conrad told me he still has feelings for me. And last night, I told Jeremiah." I let out a breath that was more like a gasp. These past couple of days had felt like weeks. I didn't even know when or how it all happened. How things got so confused. It was jumbling up in my mind, my heart.

"Oh my God," Taylor said, covering her mouth with her hands. She sank down onto the bed. "What are we going to do?"

"Conrad went looking for him." I was looking out the window again. My dad was finished with the porch, and he'd moved on to the bushes. I came away from the window and started unzipping my dress.

Startled, she said, "What are you doing?"

"You said it's going to wrinkle, remember?" I stepped out of the dress, and it slipped to the floor, a silky white puddle. And then I picked it up and put it on a hanger.

Taylor put my robe over my shoulders, and then she turned me around and tied the sash for me like I was a little girl. "It's going to be okay, Belly."

Someone knocked on the door, and both our eyes flew over to it. "It's Steven," my brother said, opening it. He came in and shut the door behind him. "Conrad got him back."

I sank onto the floor and let out a big gust of air. "He's back," I repeated.

Steven said, "He's showering, and then he'll be dressed and ready to go. Go get married, I mean. Not leave again."

Taylor knelt down next to me. Perched on her knees, she grabbed my hand and entwined my fingers with hers. "Your hand is cold," she said, warming it with her other hand. Then she said, "Do you still want to do this? You don't have to do this if you don't want to."

I squeezed my eyes shut. I had been so scared he wasn't going to go come back. Now that he was here, all the fear and panic were rising up to the surface.

Steven sat next to me and Taylor on the floor. He put his arm around me, and he said, "Belly. Take this however you want to take it, okay? I have five words for you. Are you ready?"

I opened my eyes and nodded.

Very solemnly he said, "Go big or go home."

"What the hell does that even mean, Steven?" Taylor snapped.

A laugh escaped from deep down in my chest. "Go big or go home? Go big or go home." I was laughing so hard, tears were running down my cheeks.

Taylor jumped up. "Your makeup!"

She grabbed the box of tissues on the dresser and wiped my face delicately. I was still laughing. "Snap out of it, Conklin," Taylor said, shooting a worried look at my brother. The flower in her hair was askew. She was right: the humidity wasn't doing her hair any favors.

Steven said, "Aw, she's fine. She's just having a laugh. Right, Belly?"

"Go big or go home," I repeated, giggling.

"I think she's hysterical or something. Should I slap her?" Taylor asked my brother.

"No, I'll do it," he said, advancing toward me.

I stopped laughing. I wasn't hysterical. Or maybe I was, a little bit. "I'm fine, you guys! Nobody gets to slap me. Geez." I stood up. "What time is it?"

Steven pulled his cell phone out of his pocket. "It's two o'clock. We still have a couple of hours before people get here."

Taking a deep breath, I said, "Okay. Steven, will you go tell Mom I think we should move the wedding inside? If we push the couches to the side, we can probably fit a couple of the tables in the living room."

"I'll get the other guys on it," he said.

"Thanks, Stevie. And Taylor, will you—"

Hopefully, she asked, "Stay and fix your makeup?"

"No. I was going to ask if you could get out too. I need to think."

Exchanging looks, the two of them shuffled out of my room, and I shut the door behind them.

As soon as I saw him, everything would make sense again. It had to.

chapter *fifty-four*
CONRAD

I woke up that morning to Steven shaking my bed. "Have you seen Jere?" he demanded.

"I was asleep until three seconds ago," I muttered, my eyes still closed. "How could I have seen him?"

Steven stopped shaking the bed and sat down on the edge. "He's gone, man. I can't find him anywhere, and he left his phone. What the hell happened last night?"

I sat up. Belly must have told him. Shit. "I don't know," I said, rubbing my eyes.

"What are we gonna do?"

This was all my fault.

I got out of bed and said, "Go ahead and get dressed. I'll look for him. Don't tell Belly anything."

Looking relieved, he said, "Sounds good. But shouldn't Belly know? We don't have a ton of time before the wedding. I don't want her to get ready and everything if he's not coming."

"If I'm not back in an hour, you can tell her then." I threw off my T-shirt and put on the white linen shirt Jere had made us all buy.

"Where are you gonna go?" Steven asked me. "Maybe I should go with you."

"No, you stay here and take care of her. I'll find him."

"So you know where he is, then?"

"Yeah, I think so," I said. I didn't have a clue where that bastard was. I just knew I had to fix this.

On my way out, Laurel stopped me and said, "Have you seen Jere? I need to give him something."

"He went out to get something for the wedding," I said. "I'm going to meet him now. I'll give it to him."

She handed me an envelope. I recognized the paper right away. It was my mom's stationery. Jere's name was written on the front in her handwriting. Smiling, Laurel said, "You know, I think it might be nicer this way, coming from you. Beck would like that, don't you think?"

I nodded. "Yeah, I think she would." There was no way I was coming back without Jere.

As soon as I was outside, I sprinted to my car and just gunned it out of there.

I went to the boardwalk first, then the skate park we used to hang out at as kids, then the gym, then a diner we'd stop at on the way into town. He'd always liked their strawberry milk shakes. But he wasn't there. I drove around the mall parking lot. No car and no Jere. I couldn't find him anywhere, and my hour was almost up. I was screwed. Steven was going to tell Belly, and then this would be just one more, epic time I messed up her life. What if Jere had left Cousins completely? He could be back in Boston for all I knew.

It would have been great if I had some sudden epiphany, some insight into where he was, seeing as how we were brothers. But all I could do was run down the list, every place we ever went. Where would Jeremiah go if he was upset? He'd go to my mom. But her grave wasn't here, it was in Boston.

In Cousins she was everywhere. Then it came to me—the garden. Maybe Jere had gone to the garden at the shelter. It was worth a shot. I called Steven on the way over. "I think I know where he is. Don't tell Belly anything yet."

"All right. But if I don't hear from you in half an hour, I'm telling her. Either way, I'm kicking his ass for this."

We hung up as I pulled into the women's shelter parking lot. I saw his car right away. I felt a mixture of profound relief and dread. What right did I have to say anything to him? I was the one who was responsible for this mess.

Jere was sitting on a bench by the garden, his head

in his hands. He was still in last night's clothes. His head snapped up when he heard me coming. "I'm warning you, man. Don't come near me right now."

I kept walking. When I was standing right in front of him, I said, "Come back to the house with me."

He glowered at me. "Fuck you."

"You're supposed to be getting married in a couple of hours. We don't have time to do this right now. Just hit me. It'll make you feel better." I tried to pick up his arm, and he shoved me off.

"No, it'll make *you* feel better. You don't deserve to feel better. But after the shady shit you pulled, I should beat the crap out of you."

"Then do it," I said. "And then let's go. Belly's waiting for you. Don't make her wait on her wedding day."

"Shut up!" he yelled, lunging at me. "You don't get to talk to me about her."

"Come on, man. Please. I'm begging you."

"Why? Because you still love her, right?" He didn't wait for me to answer. "What I want to know is, if you still had feelings for her, why did you give me the go-ahead, huh? I did the right thing. I didn't go behind your back. I asked you, straight up. You told me you were over her."

"You weren't exactly asking for my permission when I walked in on you kissing her in your car. Yeah, I still gave you the go-ahead, because I trusted you to take care of her and treat her right. Then you go and cheat on her in

Cabo during spring break. So maybe I should be the one asking if you love her or not." As soon as I got the last word out, Jere's fist was connecting with my face, hard. It was like getting hit with a ten-foot wave—all I could hear was the ringing in my ears. I staggered backward. "Good." I gasped. "Can we get out of here now?"

He punched me again. This time I fell to the ground.

"Shut up!" he yelled. "Don't talk to me about who loves Belly more. I've always loved her. Not you. You treated her like garbage. You left her so many times, man. You're a coward. Even now, you can't admit it to my face."

Breathing hard, I spat out a mouthful of blood and said, "Fine. I love her. I admit it. Sometimes—sometimes I think she's the only girl I could ever be with. But Jere, she picked you. You're the one she wants to marry. Not me." I pulled the envelope out of my pocket, stumbled up, and pushed it at his chest. "Read this. It's for you, from Mom. For your wedding day."

Swallowing, he tore the envelope open. I watched him as he read, hoping, knowing, my mom would have the right words. She always knew what to say to Jeremiah.

Jere started to cry as he read, and I turned my head away.

"I'm going back," he finally said. "But not with you. You're not my brother anymore. You're dead to me. I don't want you at my wedding. I don't want you in my life. I want you gone."

"Jere—"

"I hope you said everything you needed to say to her. Because after this, you're never seeing her again. Or me. It's over. You and I are done." He handed me the letter. "This is yours, not mine."

Then he left.

I sat on the bench and opened the paper up. It said, Dear Conrad.

And then I started to cry too.

chapter *fifty-five*

Outside my window, far down the beach, I could see a group of little kids with plastic pails and shovels, digging for sand crabs.

Jere and I used to do that. There was this one time, I think I was eight, which meant Jeremiah must have been nine. We'd searched for sand crabs all afternoon, and even when Conrad and Steven came looking for him, he didn't leave. They said, "We're going to ride our bikes into town and rent a video game, and if you don't come with us, you can't play tonight."

"You can go if you want," I'd said, feeling wretched because I knew he'd choose to go. Who would choose sandy old sand crabs over a new video game?

He hesitated, and then said, "I don't care." And then he stayed.

I felt guilty but also triumphant, because Jeremiah had chosen me. I was worthy of being chosen over someone else.

We played outside until it got dark. We collected our sand crabs in a plastic cup, and then we set them free. We watched them wriggle back into the sand. They all seemed to know exactly where they were going. Some clear destination in mind. Home.

That night, Conrad and Steven played their new game. Jeremiah watched them. He didn't ask if he could play, and I could see how much he wanted to.

In my memory he would always be golden.

Someone knocked on the door. "Taylor, I need a minute by myself," I said, turning around.

It wasn't Taylor. It was Conrad. He looked worn down, exhausted. His white linen shirt was wrinkled. So were his shorts. When I looked closer, I saw that his eyes were bloodshot, and I could see a bruise forming on his cheek.

I ran over to him. "What happened? Did you guys get into a fight?"

He shook his head.

"You shouldn't be in here," I said, backing away. "Jeremiah's coming up any minute."

"I know, I just need to say something to you."

I moved back to the window, turning my back on him. "You've said plenty. Just go."

I heard him turn the doorknob, and then I heard him close the door again. I thought he'd gone, until I heard him say, "Do you remember infinity?"

Slowly, I turned around. "What about it?"

Tossing something toward me, he said, "Catch."

I reached out and caught it in the air. A silver necklace. I held it up and examined it. The infinity necklace. It didn't shine the way it used to; it looked a bit coppery now. But I recognized it. Of course I recognized it.

"What is this?" I asked.

"You know what it is," he said.

I shrugged. "Nope, sorry."

I could see that he was both hurt and angry. "Okay, then. You don't remember it. I'll remind you. I bought you that necklace for your birthday."

My birthday.

It had to have been for my sixteenth birthday. It was the only year he ever forgot to buy me a birthday present—the last summer we'd all been together at the beach house, when Susannah was still alive. The next year, when Conrad took off and Jeremiah and I went looking for him, I found it in his desk. And I took it, because I knew it was mine. He took it back later. I never knew when he had bought it or why, I just knew it was mine. Hearing him say it now, that it was my birthday present, touched me in the last place I wanted him to touch me. My heart.

I took his hand and put the necklace in his palm. "I'm sorry."

Conrad held the necklace out to me. Softly, he said, "It belongs to you, always has. I was too afraid to give it to you then. Consider it an early birthday gift. Or a belated one. You can do whatever you want with it. I just—can't keep it anymore."

I was nodding. I took the necklace from him.

"I'm sorry for screwing everything up. I hurt you again, and for that I'm sorry. I'm so sorry. I don't want to do that anymore. So . . . I'm not going to stay for the wedding. I'm just going to take off now. I won't see you again, not for a long time. Probably for the best. Being near you like this, it hurts. And Jere"—Conrad cleared his throat and stepped backward, making space between us—"he's the one who needs you."

I bit my lip to keep from crying.

Hoarsely, he said, "I need you to know that no matter what happens, it was worth it to me. Being with you, loving you. It was all worth it." Then he said, "I wish you both the best. Take good care of each other."

I had to fight every instinct in me not to reach out, not to touch the bruise that was blooming on his left cheekbone. Conrad wouldn't want me to. I knew him well enough to know that.

He came up and kissed me on my forehead, and before he stepped away, I closed my eyes and tried hard to memorize this moment. I wanted to remember him exactly as he was right then, how his arms looked brown against his white shirt, the way his hair was cut a little too short in the front. Even the bruise, there because of me.

Then he was gone.

Just for that moment, the thought that I might never see him again . . . it felt worse than death. I wanted to run after him. Tell him anything, everything. Just don't go. Please just never go. Please just always be near me, so I can at least see you.

Because it felt final. I always believed that we would find our way back to each other every time. That no matter what, we would be connected—by our history, by this house. But this time, this last time, it felt final. Like I would never see him again, or that when I did, it would be different, there would be a mountain between us.

I knew it in my bones. That this time was it. I had finally made my choice, and so had he. He let me go. I was relieved, which I expected. What I didn't expect was to feel so much grief.

Bye bye, Birdie.

chapter *fifty-six*

It was Valentine's Day. I was sixteen, and he was eighteen. It fell on a Thursday that year, and Conrad had classes until seven on Thursdays, so I knew we wouldn't be going on a date or anything. We'd talked about hanging out on Saturday, maybe watching a movie, but neither of us mentioned Valentine's Day. He just wasn't a flowers and candy hearts kind of guy. No big deal. I'd never been that kind of girl either, not like Taylor was.

At school the drama club delivered roses during fourth period. People had been buying them all week during lunch. You could have them sent to whoever you wanted. Freshman year, neither of us had boyfriends, and Taylor and I secretly sent each other one. That year, her boyfriend, Davis, sent her a dozen pink ones, and he bought her a red headband she'd been eyeing at the mall. She wore the headband all day.

I was up in my room that night, doing homework, when I got a text from Conrad. It said, LOOK OUT YOUR WINDOW. I'd gone to look, thinking there might be a meteor shower that night. Conrad kept track of that kind of thing.

But what I saw was Conrad, waving at me from a plaid blanket in my front yard. I clapped my hand to my mouth and let out a shriek. I couldn't believe it. Then I jammed my feet into my sneakers, put my puffy coat over my flannel pajamas, and ran down the stairs so fast I almost tripped. I made a running leap off the front porch and into his arms.

"I can't believe you're here!" I couldn't stop hugging him.

"I came right after class. Surprised?"

"So surprised! I didn't think you even knew it was Valentine's Day!"

He laughed. "Come on," he said, leading me by my shoulders over to the blanket. There was a thermos and a box of Twinkies.

"Lie down," Conrad said, stretching out his legs on the blanket. "It's a full moon."

So I lay down next to him and looked up at the inky black sky and at that shining white moon, and I shivered. Not because I was cold, but because I was happy.

He wrapped the edge of the blanket around me. "Too cold?" he asked, looking concerned.

I shook my head.

Conrad unscrewed the thermos and poured liquid into the lid. He passed it to me and said, "It's not that hot anymore, but it might still help."

I got up on my elbows and sipped. It was cocoa. Lukewarm.

"Is it cold?" Conrad asked.

"No, it's good," I said.

Then we both lay down flat on our backs and stared up at the sky together. So many stars. It was freezing cold, but I didn't care. Conrad took my hand, and he used it to point out constellations and connect the dots. He told me the stories behind Orion's belt and Cassiopeia. I didn't have the heart to tell him I already knew; my dad had taught me those constellations when I was a kid. I just loved listening to Conrad talk. He had the same wonder in his voice, the same reverence he always had when he talked about nature and science.

"Wanna go back in?" he asked, sometime later. He warmed my hand with his.

"I'm not going in until we see a shooting star," I answered him.

"We might not," he said.

I wriggled next to him happily. "It's okay if we don't. I just want to try."

Smiling, he said, "Did you know that astronomers call them interplanetary dust?"

"Interplanetary dust," I repeated, liking the feel of the words on my tongue. "Sounds like a band."

Conrad breathed hot air on my hand, and then he put it in his coat pocket. "Yeah, it kinda does."

"Tonight, it's—the sky is like—" I searched for the right word to encapsulate how it made me feel, how beautiful it was. "Lying here and looking up at the stars like this, it makes me feel like I'm lying on a *planet*. It's so wide. So infinite."

"I knew you'd get it," he said.

I smiled. His face was close to mine, and I could feel the heat from his body. If I turned my head, we'd be kissing. I didn't, though. Being close to him was enough.

"Sometimes I think I'll never trust another girl the way I trust you," he said then.

I looked over at him, surprised. He wasn't looking at me, he was still looking up at the sky, still focused.

We never did see a shooting star, but it didn't matter to me one bit. Before the night was over, I said, "This is one of my top moments."

He said, "Mine too."

We didn't know what was ahead of us then. We were just two teenagers, looking up at the sky on a cold February night. So no, he didn't give me flowers or candy. He gave me the moon and the stars. Infinity.

chapter *fifty-seven*

He knocked on the door once. "It's me," he said.

"Come in." I was sitting on the bed. I had changed back into my dress. People would be arriving soon.

Jeremiah opened the door. He was in his linen shirt and khaki shorts. He hadn't shaved yet. But he was dressed, and his face was unmarked, no bruises. I took that as a good sign.

He sat down on the bed next to me. "Isn't it bad luck for us to see each other before the wedding?" he asked.

Relief washed over me. "So there's going to be a wedding, then?"

"Well, I'm all dressed up and so are you." He kissed me on the cheek. "You look great, by the way."

"Where did you go?"

Shifting, he said, "I just needed some time to think.

I'm ready now." Leaning toward me, he kissed me again, this time on the lips.

I drew back. "What's the matter with you?"

"I told you, it's all good. We're getting married, right? You still want to get married?" He said it lightly, but I could hear an edge in his voice I'd never heard before.

"Can't we at least talk about what happened?"

"I don't want to talk about it," Jeremiah snapped. "I don't even want to think about it again."

"Well, I do want to talk about it. I need to. I'm freaked out, Jere. You just left. I didn't even know if you were coming back."

"I'm here, aren't I? I'm always here for you." He tried to kiss me again, and this time I pushed him off.

He rubbed his jawline roughly. Then he stood up and started pacing around the room. "I want all of you. I want every part. But you're still holding back from me."

"What are we talking about here?" I asked, my voice shrill. "Sex?"

"That's part of it. But it's more than that. I don't have your whole heart. Be honest. I'm right, aren't I?"

"No!"

"How do you think it makes me feel, knowing I'm second choice? Knowing it was always supposed to be you two?"

"You're not my second choice! You're first!"

Jeremiah shook his head. "No, I'll never be first. That'll

always be Con." He hit his palm against the wall. "I thought I could do this, but I can't."

"You can't what? You can't marry me?" My mind was spinning like a top, and then I started talking, fast. "Okay, maybe you're right. It's all too crazy right now. We won't get married today. We'll just move in to that apartment. Gary's apartment, the one you wanted. I'm fine with it. We can move second semester. Okay?"

He didn't say anything, and so I said it again, this time more panicked. "Okay, Jere?"

"I can't. Not unless you can look at me right now— look me in the eyes and tell me you don't still love Con."

"Jere, I love *you*."

"That's not what I'm asking. I know you love me. What I'm asking is, do you love him too?"

I wanted to tell him no. I opened my mouth. Why wouldn't the words come out? Why couldn't I say what he needed to hear? It would be so easy to just say it. One word and this would all go away. He wanted to forgive and forget it all. I could see it in his face: all he needed was for me to tell him no. He would still marry me. If I would just say the word. One word.

"Yes."

Jere inhaled sharply. We stared at each other for a long moment, and then he inclined his head.

I stepped toward him and filled the space between us. "I think—I think I'll always love him a little bit. I'll always have him in my heart. But he's not the one I choose. I choose you, Jeremiah."

All my life, I never felt like I had a choice when it came to Conrad. Now I knew it wasn't true. I did have a choice. I chose to walk away, then and now. I chose Jeremiah. I chose the boy who would never walk away from me.

His head was still bowed. I willed him to look at me, to believe me just one more time. Then he lifted his head and said, "That's not enough. I don't just want a part of you. I want all of you."

My eyes filled.

He walked over to my dresser and picked up the letter from Susannah. "You haven't read yours yet."

"I didn't even know if you were coming back!"

He ran his finger along the edges, staring down at it. "I got one too. But it wasn't for me. It was Con's. My mom must have mixed up the envelopes. In the letter she said—she said she only ever got to see him in love once. That was with you." He looked at me then. "I won't be the reason you don't go to him. I won't be your excuse. You've got to see for yourself, or you'll never be able to let him go."

"I already have," I whispered.

Jeremiah shook his head. "No, you haven't. The worst part is, I knew you hadn't and I still asked you to marry me. So I guess I'm partly to blame too, huh?"

"No."

He acted like he didn't hear me. "He will let you down, because that's what he does. That's who he is."

For the rest of my life, I was going to remember those words. Everything Jeremiah said to me that day, our wedding day, I would remember. I would remember the words Jeremiah said and the way he looked at me when he said them. With pity, and with bitterness. I hated myself for being the one who made him bitter, because that was one thing he'd never been.

I reached up and laid my palm on his cheek. He could have pushed my hand away, he could have recoiled at my touch. He didn't. Just that one tiny thing told me what I needed to know—that Jere was still Jere and nothing could ever change that.

"I still love you," he said, and the way he said it, I knew that if I wanted him to, he would still marry me. Even after everything that had happened.

There are moments in every girl's life that are bigger than we know at the time. When you look back, you say, That was one of those life-changing, fork-in-the-road moments and I didn't even see it coming. I had no idea. And then there are the moments that you know are big. That whatever you do next, there will be an impact. Your life could go in one of two directions. Do or die.

This was one of those moments. Big. They didn't get much bigger than this.

It ended up not raining that day. Jeremiah's frat brothers and my actual brother moved the tables and chairs and hurricane vases in for nothing.

Another thing that didn't happen that day: Jeremiah and I didn't get married. It wouldn't have been right. Not for either of us. Sometimes I wondered if we had rushed into getting married because we were both trying to prove something to the other and maybe even to ourselves. But then I think no, we truly did love each other. We truly did have the best of intentions. It, we, just weren't meant to be.

a couple of years later

Dearest Belly,

Right now I am picturing you today, on your wedding day, looking radiant and lovely, the prettiest bride there ever was. I picture you about thirty or so, a woman who's had lots and lots of adventures and romances. I picture you marrying a man who is solid and steady and strong, a man with kind eyes. I am sure your young man is completely wonderful, even if he doesn't have the last name Fisher! Ha.

You know that I could not love you more if you were my own daughter. My Belly, my special girl. Watching you grow up was one of the great joys of my life.

My girl who ached and yearned for so many
things . . . a kitten you could name Margaret,
rainbow roller skates, edible bubble bath! A boy
who would kiss you the way Rhett kissed Scarlett.
I hope you've found him, darling.

Be happy. Be good to each other.

All of my love always, Susannah

Oh, Susannah. If you could see us now.

You were wrong about a couple of things. I'm not
thirty yet. I'm twenty-three, almost twenty-four. After
Jeremiah and I broke up, he went back to live in the fraternity house, and I ended up living with Anika after all.
Junior year, I studied abroad. I went to Spain, where I did
have lots and lots of adventures.

Spain is where I got my first letter from him. Real letters, written by his hand, not e-mails. I didn't write him
back, not at first, but they still came, once a month, every
month. The first time I saw him again, it was another year,
at my college graduation. And I just knew.

My young man is kind and good and strong, just like
you said. But he doesn't kiss me like Rhett kissed Scarlett.
He kisses me even better. And there's one other thing you
were right about. He does have the last name Fisher.

I am wearing the dress my mother and I picked out together—creamy white with lace cap sleeves and a low back. My hair, my hair that we spent an hour pinning up, is falling out of the side bun, and long wet strands of hair are flying around my face as we run for the car in the pouring rain. Balloons are everywhere. My shoes are off, I am barefoot, holding his gray suit jacket over my head. He's got one high-but-not-too-high heel in each hand. He runs ahead of me and opens the car door.

We are just married.

"Are you sure?" he asks me.

"No," I say, getting in. Everyone will be expecting us at the reception hall. We shouldn't keep them waiting. But then again, it's not like they can get started without us. We have to dance the first dance. "Stay," by Maurice Williams and the Zodiacs.

I look out the window, and there is Jere across the lawn. He has his arm around his date, and our eyes meet. He gives me a small wave. I wave back and blow him a kiss. He smiles and turns back to his date.

Conrad opens the car door and slides into the driver's seat. His white shirt is soaked through—I can see his skin. He is shivering. He grabs my hand, locks my fingers into his, and brings it to his lips. "Then let's do it. We're both wet already."

He turns on the ignition, and then we're off. We head for the ocean. We hold hands the whole way. When we get there, it is empty, so we park right on the sand. It's still raining out.

I jump out of the car, hitch up my skirt, and call out, "Ready?"

He rolls up his pant legs, and then he grabs my hand. "Ready."

We run toward the water, tripping in the sand, screaming and laughing like little kids. At the last second he picks me up like he is carrying me across a threshold. "If you dare try and Belly Flop me right now, you're going down with me," I warn, my arms tight around his neck.

"I go wherever you go," he says, launching us into the water.

This is our start. This is the moment it becomes real. We are married. We are infinite. Me and Conrad. The first boy I ever slow danced with, ever cried over. Ever loved.

Turn the page to read the letters
Conrad sent to Belly!

Even now, all these years later, I still read them—Conrad's letter to me when I was studying abroad in Spain. Just every once in while, I pull them all out and sit down and read each one. I know them all by heart, but they still touch me, they still make me fee it all over again. . . . To think that once we were both very young and very far apart, and still finding our way back to each other.

Dear Belly,

Firstly—I don't even know if I should be writing you, if this is allowed. I hope it's allowed. I hope you don't throw this away without even opening the box—because if you do, you'll miss out on something very important. Okay, fine, something that was once very important. To you.

I went over to your house to fix your mom's computer. I went into your room to use the printer and I saw Junior Mint sitting on the bookshelf, looking incredibly pathetic. Remember him? Polar bear, wears glasses and a very stylish scarf? I won him for you at the ring toss? Do you remember how you used to go over to the ring toss and just stare at the polar bears because you wanted one so bad? I probably spent thirty or forty bucks trying to win you that damn bear.

Apparently, he misses you irrespective of that fact that you left him behind. He feels lost without you. I'm serious, that's what he told me. Pathetic, right?

So here he is. Be nice to him, will you?

          Conrad

Dear Belly,

This is weird, writing you like this. I think the last time I wrote someone an actual letter was a thank-you card to my grandma. For graduation money, I think. My mom was big on thank-you cards. Oh, by the way, you're welcome for Junior Mint. Laur told me you said thanks. Geez, I was hoping for a thank-you card, but I guess we can't all be as polite as me. Haha.

I should be working on biochem, but I'd rather be talking to you. Laurel says your Spanish is getting better. She told me you got lost the other day trying to hunt down a pack of Sour Patch Kids. Sour Patch Kids? Really? You're too grown-up for Junior Mint but not for Sour Patch Kids, huh?

Here's the biggest bag I could find. It's economy sized. The next time I see you, I'm sure you'll be toothless. But happy. I really do hope you're happy.

Conrad

Dear Belly,

So far I've written you two letters and you've written me—well, none. . . . Which is fine. Go ahead and feel free not to write me back. Seriously, don't feel obligated or anything. Even though I've sent you two handwritten letters and two gifts. . . . But seriously, don't write back. I'm serious. It's better this way. I like hearing my news secondhand, from Laur.

Speaking of news, she told me you met some Spanish guy named Benito, and he rides around on a scooter. Really, Belly? A guy named Benito with a scooter? He probably wears leather pants and has a long stringy ponytail. I don't even want to know. Don't tell me. He probably looks like a model and weighs 100 pounds and writes you poetry in Spanish. I don't know what you see in a guy like that, but I don't know what you ever saw in me either, so I guess there's no accounting for taste, right?

Don't forget—don't write back.

Conrad

Dear Belly,

You didn't write back. I thought for sure you would, you used to be so bad at following directions, now look at you. . . . Kidding. Actually I'm not-remember that time you tried to make box potatoes au gratin and you forgot to put in the cheese?

Speaking of potatoes au gratin, your mom made some for Thanksgiving. Laurel invited us to dinner-my dad and Jere and me. I wasn't sure if Jere would come, but he did. It was awkward as hell. But then Steven put on football and we all just sat and watched and it was better. During the half, Jere asked if I'd heard from you, and I said no. He said you'd been chatting online. He said you cut your hair shorter, that it makes you look older, more mature. Then Laur showed us pictures of when she came to visit you. I want to go there some day. I heard you aren't hanging out with that guy Benito anymore. Don't say I didn't warn you. . . .

By the way, it looks good. Your hair. I don't think it makes you look older, though. Younger, if anything.

I might as well be completely honest here, because who even knows if you're reading this . . . you might have thrown it out without opening it, which is your right. But I'll go ahead and say it-it killed me a little that Jere's seen you, talked to you.

But I don't think he hates me anymore, which is the important thing.

Also—in case I haven't made it clear . . . I think about you a lot. You're pretty much all I think about. Just so we're clear.

Conrad

Dear Belly,

It's Christmas here. I guess it's Christmas where you are too. I went to the summerhouse for a few days. I kept thinking I'd turn around and see you-stuffing your face with chocolate pretzels, or sliding around the downstairs living room in those god-awful mistletoe pajama pants. I bet my mom bought them for you. She used to buy Jere and me matching Christmas sweaters. There's one horrible family portrait of all of us in red button-downs and reindeer bowties. It's basically a blight on humanity. I hid it in the attic one night and no one's seen it since. If you've been a very good girl this year, maybe I'll show you when you come back. My gift to you.

You know what you could give me? A letter back. Hell, I'll even take a postcard. Or an e-mail. Anything. I just want to hear from you. I want to know how you're doing. By the time you get this, Christmas will have passed-I hope it was a nice one.

Merry Christmas, Belly. Remember last year? Me and you at the summerhouse? Best Christmas of my life.

Love,

Conrad

Dear Conrad,

When I come home next spring, you'd better show me that family portrait. Don't you dare try to get out of it. Oh, and I'll be taking it with me, since it's my gift and all.

And yes. I do remember. Of course I remember. It was my best Christmas, too.

Write back soon,

Belly

For years he kept it in his wallet, soft and creased into a million little folds. He said it kept him going. Kept him hoping. He said he wanted to keep it with him always, but I said we should keep the letters together, where they belong. And he did show me the family photo. It's hanging up in our living room.

Jenny Han, the author of the
New York Times bestselling
THE SUMMER I TURNED PRETTY
series and Siobhan Vivian,
the acclaimed author of
THE LIST, team up for
BURN FOR BURN,
the first book in a captivating trilogy.

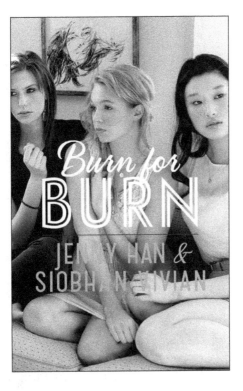

Turn the page for an exclusive sneak peek!

LILLIA

It's that time of year again, the end of August, only one more week till school starts. The beach is crowded, but not July Fourth–crowded. I'm lying on a big blanket with Rennie and Alex. Reeve and PJ are throwing a Frisbee around, and Ashlin and Derek are swimming in the ocean. This is our crew. It's been this way this since the ninth grade. It's hard to believe we're finally seniors.

The sun is so bright, I can feel my tan getting even more golden. I wriggle my body deeper into the sand. I love the sun.

Next to me Alex is putting more sunscreen on his shoulders.

"God, Alex," Rennie says, looking up from her magazine. "You need to bring your own sunscreen. You used up half my bottle. Next time, I'm just going to let you get cancer."

"Are you kidding me?" Alex says. "You stole this out of my cabana. Back me up, Lil."

I push myself up on to my elbows and sit up. "You missed a spot on your shoulder. Here, turn around."

I squat behind him and rub a dollop of sunscreen onto his shoulder. Alex turns around and asks, "Lillia, what kind of perfume do you wear?"

I laugh. "Why? Do you want to borrow it?" I love to tease Alex Lind. He's so easy.

He laughs too. "No. I'm just curious."

"It's a secret," I say, patting him on the back.

It's so important for a girl to have a signature scent. A scent everyone knows you by, so that when you walk down the hallway at school, people turn and look, like a Pavlovian response or something. Every time they smell that perfume, they'll think of you. Burnt sugar and bluebell, that's the Lillia scent.

I lie back down on the blanket and flip onto my stomach. "I'm thirsty," I announce. "Will you pass me my Coke, Lindy?"

Alex leans over and rummages through the cooler. "All that's left is water and beer."

I frown, and look over at Reeve. He's got a Frisbee in one hand, my Coke in the other. "Ree-ve!" I yell out. "That was mine!"

"Sorry," he calls back, not sounding sorry at all. He throws the Frisbee in a perfect arc, and it lands over by some cute girls sitting in beach chairs. Exactly where he wanted it to land, I'm sure.

I look over at Rennie, whose eyes are narrow.

Alex stands up and brushes sand off his shorts. "I'll get you another soda."

"You don't have to," I say. But of course I don't mean it. I really am thirsty.

"You're going to miss me when I'm not here to get your drinks," he says, grinning at me. Alex, Reeve, and PJ are going on a deep-sea fishing trip tomorrow. They'll be gone for a whole week. The boys are always around; we see them nearly every day. It will be strange to finish out the summer without them.

I stick my tongue out at him. "I won't miss you one bit!"

Alex jogs over to Reeve, and then they head off to the hot dog stand down the beach.

"Thanks, Lindy!" I call out, feeling sentimental all of a

sudden. He is so good to me.

I look back over at Rennie, who's smirking. "That boy would do anything for you, Lil."

"Stop it."

"Yes or no. Do you think Lindy's cute? Be honest."

I don't even have to think about it. "Yeah, he's obviously cute. Just not to me." Rennie has gotten it into her head that Alex and I should become a couple, and then she and Reeve can become a couple, and we can go on double dates and weekend trips together. As if my parents would ever let me go away with guys! Rennie can go ahead and get an S.T.D. from Reeve if she wants, but Alex and I are not happening. I don't see him that way, and he doesn't see me that way. We're friends. That's it. Rennie gives me a look, but thankfully she doesn't push it any further. Holding up her magazine, she asks, "What do you think about me doing my hair like this for homecoming?" It's a picture of a girl in a sparkly silver dress, her blond hair flowing behind her like a cape.

Laughing, I say, "Ren, homecoming is in October!"

"Exactly! Only a month and a half away." She waves the magazine at me. "So what do you think?"

I guess she's right. We probably should start thinking about dresses. There's no way I'm buying mine from one of the boutiques on the island, not when there's a 90% chance some other girl will show up wearing it too. I take a closer look at the picture. "It's cute! But I doubt there'll be a wind machine."

Rennie snaps her fingers. "Yes! A wind machine. Amazing idea, Lil."

I laugh. If that's what she wants, that's what she'll get. Nobody ever says no to Rennie Holtz.

We're discussing possible homecoming looks when two guys come over by our blanket. One is tall with a crew cut and the other is stockier, with thick biceps. They're both cute, although the shorter one is cuter. They're definitely older than us, definitely not in high school.

Suddenly I'm glad I'm wearing my new black bikini and not my pink and white polka-dot one.

"Do you girls have a bottle opener?" the tall one asks.

I shake my head. "You can probably borrow one from the concessions stand, though."

"How old are you girls?" the built one asks me.

I can tell Rennie is into him, the way she tosses her hair over to one side and says, "Why do you want to know?"

"I want to make sure it's okay to talk to you," he says, grinning. He's looking at her now. "Legally."

She giggles, but in a way that makes her sound older, not like a kid. "We're legal. Barely. How old are you guys?"

"Twenty-one," the taller one says, looking down at me. "We're seniors at UMass, here for the week."

I adjust my bikini top so it doesn't show so much. Rennie just turned eighteen, but I'm still seventeen.

"We're having a party tonight at our house down Shore Road in Canobie Bluffs. You should come." The built one sits down next to Rennie. "Give me your number."

"Ask nicely," Rennie says, all sugar and spice. "And then maybe I'll think about it."

The tall guy sits down next to me, at the edge of the blanket. "I'm Mike."

"Lillia," I say. Over his shoulder I see the boys coming back. Alex has a Coke in his hand for me. They're looking at us, probably wondering who these guys are. Our guy friends can be superprotective when it comes to non-islanders.

Alex frowns and says something to Reeve. Rennie sees them too; she starts giggling extraloud and tossing her hair around again.

The tall guy, Mike, asks me, "Are those guys your boyfriends?"

"No," I say. He's looking at me so intently, I blush.

"Good," he says, and smiles at me. He has really nice teeth.

I smile back.

RIVETED

BY *simon* teen ♥

BELIEVE IN YOUR SHELF

Visit RivetedLit.com & connect with us on social to:

DISCOVER NEW YA READS

READ BOOKS FOR FREE

DISCUSS YOUR FAVORITES

SHARE YOUR IDEAS

ENTER SWEEPSTAKES FOR THE CHANCE TO WIN BOOKS

Follow @SimonTeen on

to stay up to date with all things Riveted!

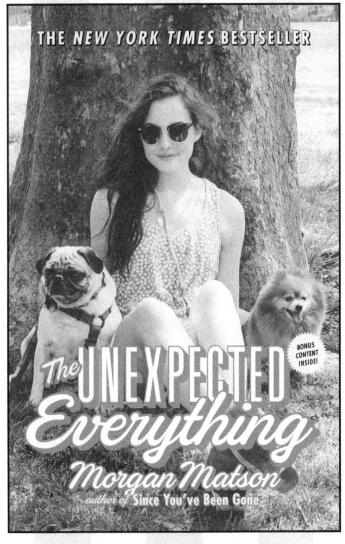 

CPSIA information can be obtained
at www.ICGtesting.com
Printed in the USA
BVHW080601200722
641338BV00002B/2

9 781416 995593